A Sinner's Circle

Church Is Where I Learned to Sin Professionally

Arketa Williams

Copyright © 2019 by Arketa Williams.

ISBN: 978-1-970135-13-8 Paperback
       978-1-970135-11-4 Hardcover
       978-1-970135-12-1 Ebook

Published in the United States by Pen2Pad Ink Publishing.

Requests to publish work from this book or to contact the author should be sent to: contact@pen2padink.org

Arketa Williams retains the rights to all images.

To Whom It May Concern,

To all of you starting out on your Christian journey, listen. Too many Christians take advantage of grace and take scriptures out of context to justify their wrong doings. They seek out the people who are new to the Christian walk. They corrupt and destroy the innocence of your body, mind and spirit before you even have a true chance to get started. Read and study your Bible. Know the word for yourself. Develop your own personal relationship with God. He knew I was so desperate for Him yet, so broken and so weary. I had completely tuned Him out and rejected Christians with a title like Bishop, Reverend, Pastor, Evangelist, etc. As you read my story, keep your eyes open and don't fall into the same traps I did as I looked for love in all the wrong places.

Church, for me, is where I learned to sin professionally. Everything I learned in the church I took out into the world and got paid for it. As far back as I can remember, going to church was better than any soap opera on television! There was always something going on and it was either extremely hurtful or highly entertaining. There was never an in between. I knew the preacher talked about a man named Jesus a lot, but I never knew much about Him. I knew more stories about the members than I did the Bible. That's just how it was.

Everyone has a story to tell but this one is mine. Allow me to introduce myself. My name is Karen Monique Mooreland. I was born in Carmel, Indiana at Brooklyn Field Memorial. I came into this world fighting and I've been fighting ever since. My most horrific fights came from church therefore, church will always look different in my eyes. I didn't understand its purpose other than the pain caused by the pimps in the pulpit. The longer I went the more I noticed that I didn't see church the same way everybody else did. It carried a huge portion of my hurt and pain. I learned more about the people and how to survive than I did about Jesus.

I became accustomed to being a part of the pew ministry, listening to the tales of the pew, but I never thought those tales would become my real-life story. As much as I said I would never do or never be, I became all that and then some. My advice to others now is to never say never because there's always a possibility. I spent my life desiring two things. One, to be loved and two, to know Jesus. This is my journey to finding them both. I remember it just like it was yesterday…

Karen

Chapter 1

My mama was a praying woman who believed in sending me to church whether she went or not. Since I had spent most of my life in and out of church, when I turned 12 she started sending me by myself. Every Sunday my mama would wake me up and make me get dressed. I'd walk down the street to Burning Bush Missionary Baptist Church. Just talking about it, I can still see that little white building with the brown trim around it sitting on the corner. It was this little hole in the wall church a couple blocks up the road. If you weren't careful you'd miss it. Though I liked a few people there I couldn't stand that church. However, I tried to make the best of the situation. The old preyed on the young and everything was either a fight or a competition. Despite what was going on there I went because it was instilled in me to go. It was a ritual I was accustomed to. Church was the place I could go to for a few hours, get free entertainment then go back to my life.

Early one Sunday morning as I walked down the street, the hot sun shined brightly on my face. The wind was blowing a soft cool breeze. The leaves on the trees were gently swaying back and forth. I smiled as I strolled along because this was a big day for me. My mom was actually coming to church with me today. I was so excited! She'd bought me a beautiful long cream dress. It had long sleeves with perfectly shaped circular holes along each arm that reminded me of a pair of fishnet stockings. It clung to me like a glove. It wasn't inappropriate, but it definitely showed that my body was maturing. I think it even shocked my mom to realize how developed I was. I think she was going to tell me to take it off but changed her mind as she watched my face light up as I twirled around in the mirror. I felt beautiful, like a real teenager! My heart was full of jitters because it was my turn to give the speech on behalf of my Sunday school class.

I had made sure to study the lesson and knew the answers to all the recap questions. I even practiced the summary I had written. My speech was going to be delivered with confidence and pride. I was ready! When my mom and I walked into the church, all eyes were on us. I wasn't surprised. We were beautiful and my mom always commanded attention everywhere she went. She had a gorgeous peanut-butter complexion, slender build, a pair of hefty perfectly perky boobs, and a strut that made you move to the side as she sashayed by. My mother was a short woman around 5'0 feet tall. It's funny… I remember she was so short she had to sit on a pillow so she could see over the steering wheel.

Yet, this Sunday the atmosphere felt different… strange even. But, I couldn't figure out what it was. We went off to our Sunday school classes. My mom was with the adults and I was with the juniors. At the end of class each group gathered in the Sanctuary to give the speech on what the lesson was about. I waited patiently until it was my turn. When I walked up to the front of the church I felt a weird energy. I noticed the men in the church were smiling at me but the women were looking at me like they wanted me to sit down. I tried hard to ignore how weird it felt and focus on my lesson. I remembered what my mom told me before we left the house. 'Stand up straight, take your time, pronounce your words correctly, and speak with authority'. She said I was a representative of God's words. As such, I had no reason to be afraid so I better not sound like I was. I delivered the lesson just as she'd instructed and received an enormous applause and encouraging compliments from everyone. I was on cloud nine. I knew I made God and my mom proud. During announcements, one of the members said we were going to be having a meeting after church in the basement and that all the women and their children should attend.

Well, apparently my dress, or I should say, "Appropriate church attire" was the topic of discussion. Some of the older women felt that the developing teenage girls in the church should not wear clothes that were deemed "a little too much for church" because it was sending the boys and men the wrong impression. I was taught a child should stay in a child's place so I did not speak during the meeting. However, my mother spoke boldly.

"We are here to serve the Lord and not to feed into petty insecurities. I'm the judge of my children's wardrobe and will decide what is appropriate and what isn't. Maybe the problem doesn't lie with the young girls that are developing beautifully in God's image. Maybe it lies in the lustful eyes of those who need to focus more on the word instead of acting like pedophiles glaring at young children".

I was so proud she attended church with me that day. Some of the other woman were not happy with my mom's comments but did not dare come back at her or the others in her corner. But, of course, there was one who just wouldn't let it go. Sister Bigsby named off several of us girls whom she thought were too well endowed for our ages… as if we could control how our bodies grew. I remember how nasty the tone of her voice was when she spoke.

"They should be ashamed and should feel convicted enough to want to wear oversized clothes so that their features aren't so noticeable." Before I knew it all hell broke loose!

"Sister Bigsby you're the biggest hypocrite I ever seen. Sluts have no right to talk about how conservative anyone should be! We all know you're fucking the Pastor and now you wanna act holier than the rest. Just because the Pastor's dick is up in you doesn't mean you're now one with the Holy Spirit!" Sister Jones said.

"I know that's right" Sister Smith chimed in.

"BITCH!" Sister Bigsby screamed as she lunged forward. She pulled off Sister Jones wig, spit on her and slapped her in the face. She was so pissed for having just been outted that she forgot she was pretending to be saved. Sister Bigsby, Sister Jones, and Sister Smith were standing up and calling names with fists swinging, hair pulling, weave flying...

Right when it was getting good, my mother swooped me up and took me upstairs to the sanctuary. The Pastor, church Deacons, and other men flew downstairs to break up the brawl. The Pastor took control of his flock. He reprimanded the women for their behavior in God's House and in front of us. He said that everyone was to go home pray, cool down, eat and return to the church at six o'clock for a meeting to clear the air.

At six o'clock everyone was reconvening at the church. That was the first time I could remember everyone being on time for church. Once in the sanctuary, the pastor instructed everyone under the age of eighteen to go down to the lower level. He told the juniors that they were in charge of the Angels. He instructed us to put on the Bible Story video, pass out snacks to everyone and make sure we were all on our best behavior. We did exactly as we were told. Once we settled the little kids down, some of us older kids snuck over to the stairs to listen to the adults in the sanctuary.

At first, everything seemed normal. When, all of a sudden, the calm voices turned into a shouting match. We couldn't see anything but we heard everything. The first lady's voice rang out over all the others and she demanded to know if the accusations were true. The church became eerily quiet. I heard the voice of the man I admired all my life say… "I love you all deeply, but I am human and I have sinned. Sister Bigsby and I have had an affair, but I am truly in love with my wife and the Lord." Immediately the outpour of crying women who felt betrayed by their leader filled the walls of the sanctuary. The deacon board called for the Pastor's immediate removal. Our church was never the same again.

After a while we got a new Pastor and things seemed to be stable again. Since I enjoyed singing, I decided to join the youth choir. I met some new friends and the youth Pastor was really cool. He would often hold meetings with us to talk about life and upcoming events. He took us on outings and gave us special gifts. As time passed, I grew very fond of him. I would talk to him about any problems I was having and he often offered a comforting ear. Around the age of fourteen and a half, I started thinking about losing my virginity to my first love Markus Harris. He was a 6'3, muscular, red-bone. I fell for him the first moment I laid eyes on him. We had been dating for about a year and I was in love but confused. I really needed to talk to someone and I knew my mom was not an option. She would kill me and well, like most teenagers, I also thought she wouldn't understand. No parent ever understands why their child doesn't want to wait until their married to have sex. My mom would look at me differently once I was ruined. I thought she would possibly not love me anymore. Or, would think I was just as bad as Sister Bigsby. I couldn't risk losing her love. I needed to be perfect for her.

However, Pastor Jenson never judged me so I felt comfortable turning to him. We told him we needed to talk with him privately and he agreed to meet with us just before rehearsal on Tuesday. He met us at the door, we walked into one of the Sunday school class rooms and took a seat.

"So, what's going on?"

"Markus' parents will be going out of town this weekend and we're thinking about meeting at his house to do it."

"DO what?

"You know IT…"

"You mean have sex?"

"Yeaaaahhhh that's what I said IT but I'm nervous!"

He shook his head but listened with an open mind just as I expected he would.

He kept asking us to go into detail. Though somewhat confused by the line of questions, we answered them in hopes that he would be able to help us sort things out. He wanted to know exactly what the plan was, step by step. He was very interested in the positions we planned to have sex in and everything. I noticed that his breathing became slightly heavier as we answered the questions.

"Karen, have you ever cum before?" he asked. I didn't know how to respond because I didn't know what that meant. I guess he sensed, through my silence, that I was clueless. He took a deep breath,

"listen often times we do things that we are not ready for without knowing all the aspects and repercussions of our actions. Your feelings aren't wrong, but you should consider waiting until you are really ready for that type of relationship. If you are so afraid to tell your parents you want to have sex imagine how hard it would be to tell them that you got pregnant or had a sexually transmitted disease". We agreed with him and promised we would wait.

Chapter 2

A few months later my mother started getting sick. It was to the point where she was no longer able to do anything on her own. She could no longer walk, sit up, stand… Nothing. She spoke and cried. I hid my tears in an attempt to be strong for her. I stopped going to church. I tried my best to take care of her but always felt like I wasn't doing enough. Making her soup, walking it slowly over to her, watching it carefully, trying not to spill any of it. Spoon feeding her wondering if she was getting enough in her system. Struggling not to drop the bowl on her as I wiped the drippings from her chin. I felt like I needed to be doing more to make her well but I had no clue what that more should've been.

Hearing her yell out in pain, watching her struggle to move, and rubbing her back as she gasped for air while she vomited, grew more and more difficult to witness. I felt helpless but I wanted so bad to help her. I NEEDED to help her. The moments I watched as she slept gave me peace because she wasn't hurting. Watching her suffer was unbearable. I hated seeing her in so much pain and not knowing what to do was driving me crazy. I had to figure out how to take her pain away. The fact that I couldn't caused me to sometimes get frustrated and it showed. My mama thought I was mad at her and would apologize for being a burden. I told her I wasn't mad at her. I was just mad at the situation. I couldn't understand how one minute she was fine and the next minute she couldn't do anything for herself. I needed her to be well again.

When I was going to church I was taught to pray. I

was told that no matter where I was or what the situation, God would always hear me and fix any problem. So, I prayed with her and over her every day. Some days it was multiple times a day in hopes that she would start feeling better. I even declared her healed 'in Jesus name' like they did in church, desperate for it to work. The days seemed to be never ending. One rolled right into the next, seeming to be longer and worse than the day before. She wasn't getting any better. My confusion, hurt, and frustration began to grow. Why wasn't God answering me? She was getting worse, not better. This isn't what we talked about. She was supposed to be getting better!

All of a sudden, in the midst of my rollercoaster of emotions, there seemed to be a ray of hope! She was up and moving more on her own, eating a bowl of soup, smiling, and holding a conversation. I thought God had finally answered my prayers and I was so excited! Grateful couldn't even begin to describe how I was feeling. I was overjoyed! I thought my prayers had really done something. I thanked Him that whole day for what looked like a miracle. She was finally getting better. I was looking forward to us hanging out when she fully recovered.

Unfortunately, when I woke up the next morning she was back in the same state she had been in before. She was unable to do anything on her own again. She couldn't walk, she could barely move and she was in an unbearable amount of pain. She had been to the hospital twice and they said she was just having really bad muscle spasms. I was so angry and agitated. I stormed out the house looked up at the sky and screamed.

"GOD WHAT HAPPENED? YOU WERE SUPPOSED TO MAKE HER BETTER! SHE WAS BETTER AND NOW SHE'S SICK AGAIN! WHAT HAPPENED? FIX IT! FIX HER! I NEED HER TO BE BETTER".

Tears rolled down my face as I tried to calm myself

down. I straightened up, took a deep breath and walked back in the house. My mother and I started arguing because she kept apologizing for being sick. She said she knew it was taking its toll on me. She was sorry for being such a burden. She continued to think I didn't love her anymore because I was upset and scared. I don't think she believed me when I said I'd love her forever and always. I kept trying to explain to her that it wasn't her and that I was just disappointed with the situation. I was praying for her healing, thought she was getting better, and couldn't understand how we ended up back at square one. The argument ended with her telling me that "no matter what happens in life… pray". I kissed her and held her close as the tears sliding down our cheeks merged together as they fell. I continuously whispered in her ear that I loved her, needed her, and how much she meant to me.

The following morning, I walked into the living room and found her lying dead on the living room floor. Her eyes were open and looking up at the ceiling. I kneeled down to put my finger by her nose but felt no air. Instantly, I began running screaming for anybody that could hear me, begging for someone to help her. Frantically I yelled "My mama's dead! Somebody help her! My mama's dead!" In a matter of seconds my world was turned upside down. From that moment on life would never be the same for me.

The police came and sent everyone outside. I paced back and forth on her best friend's porch as I waited, praying she would come limping out the door. I needed them to help her find her breath again but that moment never came. Instead, a van pulled up that read *Coroner*. Though I saw it I still expected her to breathe again. A man got out, walked through my front door and came out with my mom's body in a bag, riding on a stretcher. I stood and watched as he rolled her from the house, placed her in the back of the van and drove away. I tried to convince myself that they were just taking her to the hospital to make her breathe again and that she would be back.

My best friend was just rolled away and I already missed her like crazy. I needed her to hurry up and return to me. I didn't fully grasp what was happening but I was devastated none the less. I watched and listened as the family gathered outside. I was still looking for her and waiting on her to show up at the front door the same way she did any other day. People told me she was in a better place and that God needed her back, but I needed her too! So, I waited for her to come home.

I spent years watching the window and walking down the street in search of my mother. I went to her friends' houses checking to see if she was there. I desperately needed to see her. I needed to tell her again how much I loved her and I needed her to understand it with no doubts. I needed her to explain life to me. I needed her to pray with me, make sure I took my medications, talk to me about the changes my body was going through, explain the emotional changes, periods, and sex… I needed her to…. My birthday, awards banquets and graduation were coming up. I needed her to be there. Who was going to help me get ready for prom when the time came? What about my wedding? If she didn't come back she'd miss that too. Who was going to be with me when I gave birth to my first child? Who was going to coach me on raising my baby? Who was going to talk to me about my first love when I met him? I NEEDED HER… I NEEDED MY MAMA… There was so much of my life I wanted to share with her. God couldn't have her! That's not what I meant when I asked Him for His help.

The day my mother died my family fell apart too. We were close. Family dinners every Sunday were a ritual at our house. My mom would cook so much food she not only fed our family but everyone went home with a plate. Even the families in the neighborhood who didn't have enough food would come by to get meals to last through the week. The days leading up to the funeral, our doors remained unlocked and open. We had a revolving door of people floating in and out our house paying respect. A decision that till this day I regret. Family came in and stole all her clothes, shoes and jewelry. The only thing I was able to keep of hers was the rose that was to be placed on her casket.

Fights erupted as lies began to spread like wildfire because of speculations surrounding her death. Since the lies were better than the truth, the fights continued in the church the day of the funeral. I attended her funeral but it still didn't sink in that she might be gone forever. I went to stay with other family members as I continued to wait on her to appear but she never showed up again.

The family grew more and more distant every day. When we did see each other it was as if the closeness we once had was buried alongside my mother. We were now strangers trying to coexist until the family just became nonexistent altogether. Struggling to emotionally cope with our new reality and unable to remain stable, we began living our own lives. Since we were just co-existing it made the departure from one another easy. There was no longer a glue in place to keep us together.

My mama was my first real lesson in heartbreak and the lessons became consistent and continuous after her death. Looking for love, acceptance, comfort, and answers, I eventually went to live with my aunt and uncle… the esteemed Pastors Timothy and Tonya Spencer and my cousin Taylor in Chickasaw, Kentucky. They pastored Saints of Shekinah Unified Body of Believers Missionary Baptist Church (SOSUBBMBC). It was the largest church in Kentucky. I thought if I went to be around family again, life would make more sense. They had been talking to me for a while about coming down but I never went. This time, their promises of unconditional love and guidance sounded like words of comfort to me. Maybe they could provide me with the answers to all my questions. Leaving my boyfriend and my friends was the second hardest thing I ever had to do.

Chapter 3

Living with my aunt and uncle was a whole lot different from how I grew up. My uncle was very affectionate and always wanted to talk. We'd sit around for hours and talk about life. They were always throwing out scenarios to see what I would do in different situations. They said they were trying to get a feel for where my head was. You never knew what kind of scenario they were going to throw at you but it always made you think outside the box. It was like *Survivor*… the mental version. I had only been living with them about a month and half before life would take its next drastic shift.

My aunt and uncle decided to have a party. A good, old-fashion cook out! I was a little excited because I was a fan of bar-b-que and was looking forward to hanging out with all my family and new friends. Everywhere I looked there were large tin pans of ribs, rib tips, burgers, buns, brats, polish, chicken, and a multitude of different side items to choose from spread out across the kitchen counters and dining room table. The adults had the entire upstairs and outside. All the teenagers and young adults partied hard in the basement. Music blaring, laughter roaring, arms waiving... we were having a fantastic time! Some of my older cousins came down and threw in a twist.

"Aye! All ya'll should have a dance contest!"

"What do we get if we win?" My cousin Shawnna asked.

"The winner receives $10 per win."

We all started high fiving each other. Everybody thought they were the best dancers anyway so this was going to be a good competition. We each paired off into five teams of two. The winner from each group was to battle one another. That meant you won $10 for beating the person you paired with, leaving five winners. Then all five of those winners went against each other, giving you the potential to gain an additional $40 if you outshined everybody else. I had seen everybody else dance before so I knew I had this in the bag, but none of the ones who were my age knew I could dance. I was normally the one who stood against the wall laughing and watching everybody else.

One by one each person started dancing. I was paired with my cousin's best friend Autumn. She was perceived to be the best dancer down there. We were the last group to go and I let her dance first. I watched with confidence as she bent over with her hands on her knees, popping and rotating her booty in a circle. Dancing to *Freak Nasty's* song *When I Dip You Dip* with everybody cheering her on, she just knew she had the win. That was until I hit floor. Smiling from ear to ear I walked up to her.

"That was real cute. Now step aside so I can teach you how it's really done" I taunted.

"Uh Oh! Somebody done gave the wall flower some confidence. This scared little lion done finally found some courage. Too bad it ain't gone be enough."

"I was never scared. It just wasn't time to school you yet. So, have several seats little girl! Grab yo pen and paper cause you gone need to take some notes!"

Laffy Taffy began to play and I started with the same moves she did. Only… I was poppin' twice as hard before droppin' into a full split while still poppin'. Then, I brought my legs behind me in a dog like position and began bouncin' my butt up and down on the floor while shakin' it in a circle. A roar of screams and laughs exploded.

Screams of "Get that SHIT! That's my cousin!"

"Yea cuz! Tear that shit up!"

belted out over the music. Still rolling in a circle while sliding up from my hands and knees until I was in a full standing position. I kept rotatin' my hips while poppin' in a diamond formation. No one knew the adults had come downstairs and was watching us compete until my uncle came all the way down and stood directly on my back as I danced so that I would be grinding against him.

"AAAWWW SHIT… Get it baby! That's my niece!" he yelled as he dropped ones, fives, and tens on top of my head. I stopped dancing and jumped out the way. Everyone stopped cheering and stared at him in disbelief. It felt so unnatural. Instantly I felt dirty. I sat down on the couch and didn't move. My cousin Misty yelled "take ya drunk, perverted ass back upstairs with all the other adults!"

Then she picked up all the cash from the floor and the money I won and handed it to me.

"You did great little cuz! I'm proud of you! Don't be embarrassed. You tow that shit up, but just watch yourself around him. You good though" she said.

"Ok and thanks…"

We didn't say anything else about it. Though I felt good about having money in my pocket I couldn't get over feeling dirty like I had just done something wrong. Everyone went on as if that moment didn't happen but no one actually danced after that. We all just sat around, laughed and talked for the rest of the night.

The next night when I went in to their room to say my usual goodnights my aunt and uncle were already in the bed laying down. I hugged and kissed my aunt then walked around to the other side of the bed to hug him. Instead, we ended up in a full-blown conversation. I took a seat on the floor on his side but watched my aunt in the mirror as we conversed. Since I was a little girl we always had open and honest conversations. We talked about God and where I was spiritually, which I thought was nowhere. I thought I didn't have a spirit and that God didn't love me because if he did, he wouldn't have punished me by taking my mother away. My uncle looked at my aunt who shook her head then changed the subject. We began talking about my future and what I wanted to do with my life.

Mid-stream my aunt said she was tired and going to sleep on us so, I stood up and went to hug my uncle goodnight. He grabbed my head. His dry hands felt like sandpaper scratching me as he cupped both sides of my face. He gripped me tight and pulled my lips towards his. What the hell? He was trying to kiss me! "Eeewwww… you nasty!" I tried to pull away but the more I pulled back the tighter his grip got. He began pulling me onto the bed closer and closer he forced me toward him with his lips poked out trying to reach mine. Trying to get free of his hands that were tightening became more and more difficult. The few minutes we struggled seemed like an eternity then he let go. I jumped off the bed and saw my aunt's eyes in the mirror. She watched everything and said nothing. I couldn't believe the look of disgust on her face as she glared back at me.

I ran out of their room and upstairs into my own. I couldn't process what had just happened but I was scared to think what might happen next. I felt trapped because I had nowhere else to go. We were family. Did that not matter? Is this why they wanted me here? You don't do that with your family AND your wife is lying right next to you! That's so disrespectful! My mind was racing all over the place and like always, I had no one to tell. Why wouldn't she help me? She saw me struggling to pull away but she just lay there… still… When I wanted to be wanted I didn't mean like this! I tried to quiet my mind enough to fall asleep but couldn't. Instead, I just lay awake, staring at the four canary yellow walls that surrounded me.

The next few days I walked on pins and needles around the house. My aunt declared a silent war blaming me for what happened. My uncle continued to make passes at me. I listened as she talked about me on the phone to her armor bearer, Sister Mattie Johnson.

"I regret ever taking her in but now I understand exactly why nobody else wanted her ass. This little bitch runnin' around here actin' like a little hoe and got one foot out the door and don't even realize it. I'll be damned if some little young tramp come runnin' up and through here tryna take over my house! Ain't no bitch gone come in here and run my house. I bind that spirit up in Jesus name! Jesus better get her before I kill her cause I'm sick of this hoe! Now I'm tryna stay calm but she pissin' me off."

I don't know what Sister Johnson said on the other end but when she came to the house later on that day she said

"Little girl… you betta watch yo self. I got my eye on you."

"Yea Ok" I replied.

I tried to stay clear of my aunt. My uncle told me not to worry about her she was all talk no action, but I was scared of them both. Fear had a new found meaning to me. My heart dropped down into my stomach but I could still feel it beating. I had a lump in my throat I couldn't get rid of. I jumped at every noise I heard during the night. As I tried to sleep my eyes would pop open with each sound. I'd quickly scan the room to see if anyone was lurking in the darkness or if anything moved. My uncle kept coming in and out of my room. He said he was just checking on us. We're not babies so why does he need to check on us so much? More often than not when I opened my eyes he was standing there. If he wasn't standing in the corner watching me he was standing over me.

So, I trained myself to identify images in the darkness that didn't belong in the room. A lot of the time, I wondered what he'd actually do to me if I stayed sleep while he was in there. I wished I could sleep like my cousin did. She was an extremely heavy sleeper and it was really hard to wake her up. Not me though. I spent many nights lying awake, watching the sun come up, too scared to close my eyes. I stopped talking to everyone. I was so uneasy. My nerves were on edge. I felt like the only safety I had resided within the four walls of this room and I tried to stay in it as much as possible. I didn't have much of an appetite so I rarely made an appearance at the dinner table. When I did, I barely ate because I was scared my food was poisoned.

Then one night it seemed like the later it was getting the hotter my room became. My mouth felt like I was sucking on a piece of sandpaper. Then my throat began feeling like I was swallowing little pebbles until I could barely form spit to swallow. I needed water so bad but I didn't want to go downstairs alone. The heat felt like a plastic bag being placed over my head, choking me. It was killing me. I kept trying to wake my cousin to go with me but she was dead to the world and wouldn't get up. I was scared to go alone but the heat was kicking my butt. It was too hot in there and the windows won't open. I think they did that on purpose. How do you work in construction and your windows don't open? That doesn't make any sense. Ok, I can't take it anymore. I keep coughing and the cough is getting worse. I'm going to have to pull my big girl panties up and go get me some water before I choke to death. Then I did it.

I stood up, quietly walked out my room, did a quick scan of the hallway before proceeding and went downstairs to get some water. I felt the hairs on the back of my neck stand up and my stomach started doing summer salts. That's when I realized I was in trouble. I got caught! He snuck up from behind. I didn't even hear him coming. All of a sudden he's moving against me. His hand around my throat… him rubbing against me from behind. I should never know what he feels like. I tried to do everything right but man my life… My cup fell. I think I stopped breathing… my words… my voice… gone. I couldn't move. I was petrified. He turned me around to face him. He stood there naked in an open robe with his boxers around his ankles. I couldn't hide my fear. Filled with regret and disappointment I stood engulfed in terror, searching for a quick escape. There was none. I should've stayed upstairs. I should've died from the heat because this is worse. I hate myself for not being stronger. I…

With his hand pulling at my pajama pants I could hear the thin material tearing. I push and scratch at him but he doesn't move. He just holds my hands together with one of his hands. Gripping tighter and tighter the more I move, my wrists are hurting and throbbing. Pains shooting from them so piercingly I thought they were going to break. My arms are pressing into my own chest as he's kissing my neck. I try again to push him off me. Using my elbows and my forearm doesn't work. He just pushes me harder into the counter. He takes his knee, thigh, and free hand and force my legs open. I manage to get them closed again, still fighting him. He opened my legs again and stuck his fingers underneath my panties. The last thread snaps.

I feel him forcing his way in. The frame of the counter is digging into my back as he begins digging in my front. As he pushes his way inside me, pains begin shooting into my body, I scream. I can taste the saltiness from my hot tears as they fall faster down my face into my mouth. Nothing is blocking out the pain. The house is quiet. Why did he do this to me? They were supposed to love me? Jesus HELP! I attempt to push him again but he continues. I can hear him moaning as he whispers in my ear.

"I always knew you'd feel good. I've been dreaming of this moment ever since you were a little girl."

"Please Stop!" The words fell off my lips between gasps of air, deep sobs and extreme pain.

"Don't you know that this was God's will. The bible says all things work together for the good of those that love him. We working together in this thing. See when you do stuff in His will He'll supply your needs. It was meant for you to be in this kitchen right now. God knew I needed some pussy and at the very moment I said it to Him he sent you to me. It was meant to be baby so just enjoy it with me. I'm ministering to your soul right now. Relax..." He grunts and moans louder.

"Please..." The words stumble off my lips again.

"I love it! Keep begging me for more. Say please again."

My tears never stopped. I should've never come here. I should've never trusted them. None of them. I gotta get outta here. GOD.... Why? Why is this happening to me? I just wanted some water... I just... Jesus help me. All of a sudden I heard the floor boards creaking. Jesus please let that be someone coming so he can stop! I hear the noise again. I think someone's coming so I begin looking into the shadows hoping to see something. Hoping they'd help me. He stopped and moved away from me. I ran. I ran to my room, closed the door, and sat in the corner all night watching the shadows. Praying I didn't see any more images in the darkness. I sat hoping that since he got what he wanted he'd leave me alone.

Again, I watched the sun come up and listened quietly to see who was moving around. When I heard it was my aunt I got up, ran to the bathroom, cut the water on, sat in the shower and cried in my towel till I could cry no more. Hoping the water would drown out the sound of my tears, I cried. Then I attempted to scrub the filthiness I felt away. It never went anywhere though. I scrubbed till my skin began to pull apart in places that weren't already separated. I still couldn't make it go away. It was like the dirt of last night rooted itself deep into my skin and rejected the water. I desperately needed to make it disappear but it wouldn't go nowhere. I could still feel his hands holding me. I could still feel his penis stabbing my insides. I tried to make it go down the drain like the water but it wouldn't go. The filth just clung to me like splattered poop to the side of the toilet. We were inseparable. I heard a knocking at the door. I jumped but didn't respond.

"Who's in the bathroom?" I heard him ask.

"It's your favorite" my aunt replied.

I quickly cut the water off, dried as fast as I could, jumped into my clothes and ran out the bathroom directly into my aunt. She was beyond pissed off at me.

"Sorry…"

"You show as hell are!" She snapped back.

"What's wrong? Why are you so mad? What did I do?" Her response told me she knew everything and she hated me for it.

"You got one foot out the door and too dumb to even realize it. You ain't shit! You'll never be shit and you'll never amount to shit. You walk around here acting like you better than everybody else if you don't get the fuck away from me I'm gone beat yo ass! You ain't shit but a sorry, nasty ass hoe and that's exactly how I'm gone treat you from now on."

I stared at her in shock and disbelief. My heart was racing. Questions rapidly fired off in my head. What did I do to be a hoe? When did I become one? What does she see in me that I don't? I hadn't even had sex before last night. My uncle took my virginity without my consent. Lost inside my head, filled with roaming thoughts, I refocused just enough to hear her confirm.

"Oh, and by the way bitch, watch ya back because I saw ya nasty ass fucking MY HUSBAND in MY KITCHEN last night! Now go bleach my fucking counters so I can cook!"

My uncle steps out the bathroom and says, "Baby you can't be mad about that. God loves a cheerful giver and I was just doing my due diligence. I was being fruitful in hopes that it multiplies." He laughed and stepped back inside the bathroom.

"Shut the hell up! You make me so fucking sick!"

"But you love me though" he taunted.

"Shut the hell up! I'm not talking to you." She rolls her eyes at him, turns back to me and says "You gone fucking pay for this. Mark my words and believe what I tell you."

"Yes Ma'am…"

I dropped my head, turned around and did as she initially instructed. I cleaned the counters then the kitchen. She cooked. I stayed in my room as they ate because I believed what she told me. Poisoning my food would be one way to make me pay. I cleaned the kitchen again when they finished. As I cleaned I did the only thing I knew to do. I was told to talk to God just like you talk to your friend. So, that's what I did. I prayed.

Dear God,

She hates me now. She said she'd love me forever but forever wasn't that long. I didn't ask for any of this. Why did you take my mama away from me? Why is my life so messed up? Why is this happening? What am I supposed to do? He was in places he wasn't supposed to be. I didn't want him there. I feel like this is my fault because I should've stayed in my room. I should've toughed it out. You saw I was scared. Why didn't you protect me? He was stronger than me.

My aunt walked into the kitchen. I jumped back as she walked up on me.

"This is your fault…. This is all your fault… you got what you were asking for and you gone get what's coming to you. I'm gone make sure of it." She walked out.

God,

When did I ask for this? How did I ask for this? I gotta get out of here. I'm gone come up missing. They tryna kill me. I gotta get outta here. I gotta get out of here but I don't have anywhere to go. If you love me help me.

Chapter 4

Once I finished the kitchen we left for the nursing home to visit the elderly. My family was big on giving back and helping others. The car ride over was quiet. I stared out the window as Donald Lawrence and the Tri-City singers' song *Love the Hurt Away* blared from the speakers. My aunt cried softly as we drove down the road. I felt so trapped and there was nothing I could do. I tried to focus on the words in the song in hopes that it could bring the parts of me that felt dead inside back to life but… I got nothing. I cried in silence. The last few months had been a lot to take in. I felt like more and more of my life was being strangled out of me daily. My aunt looked at me and spoke.

"Little girl, you better suck it up and get over it. Life happens to everybody. What's done is done and ain't no tears gone fix the damage that's been done. So, ain't no sense in crying about it now. You wasn't crying when it happened".

"Oh, but I was. I didn't ask for this" I replied.

"Yea, well in life you get what you get and you get over it".

Confused… I looked at her, let out a deep sigh and stared back out the window. I guess I didn't have a right to feel how I felt. Maybe even though I didn't verbally ask for it, it was still my fault. When we pulled up to the first nursing home she passed me a napkin.

"Here. Straighten up… and you better not embarrass me!"

I wiped my face and walked in. As we entered the door we were instantly greeted by smiles from a group of nurses.

"Hello Pastor Spencer. It's great to see you! I see you have company today."

"Yes, this is my dead sister's daughter. I was the only one willing to take her in and I'm trying to teach her to be appreciative that she has someone like me. Say hello".

"Hello" I reply in a dry tone.

She firmly griped my arm and whispered in my ear "don't forget what I told you. You better not embarrass me cause if you show yo ass I'm gonna show mine". I smiled at the ladies and spoke cheerfully "Hello Good Morning". My heart was shattered and you want me to smile and pretend everything is OK! I was doing my best to stay in her good graces. I felt like I had to make things up to her for causing so much disruption in her house. My aunt and the nurses continued to talk as I stood quietly listening.

"Yea boy I tell you… she's a hand full too! I don't know how my sister handled this little feisty package right here. But I'll get her in line if it's the last thing I do."

I tried to keep smiling all while fighting back the tears, but one slipped out. I quickly wiped it away and continued to force out a smile.

"Well if you'd like, I'm about to do my rounds. I can take her with me and have her help me out" said one of the nurses. My aunt just stared at her.

Lord,

If you up there listening please let her say yes. I've had about as much of her as I can handle right now. And can you work on someone else wanting me and get me away from them?

"That'll be fine". She grabbed my arm again snatching me close to her. This time she dug her nails into the back of my arm. I dropped my head tears started falling again. She whispered "What goes on in our house is our business. We got a reputation to maintain so don't try to ruin it. Besides ain't nobody gone believe you no way. Everything you do and say gone come back to me. I got eyes everywhere. Let this be the last time I tell you to fix yo got damn face." The more she talked the more she dug her nails into my arm. Then she released her grip, smiled, kissed my cheek and told me to behave.

"Hello sweetheart. My name is Jacquetta. What's your name?" She extended her hand.

"Karen" I extended mine and we shook hands.

"It's a pleasure to meet you. Are you ok?"

"I'm ok". I continued walking with my head down.

"Are you sure?" I didn't say anything. I just looked up at her.

"Where are your parents?"

"My mom died a few months ago and my dad is back home in Carmel, Indiana".

"Oh, I'm sorry. And you're sure you're ok?"

"Why? I mean, I'm not trying to get smart or anything. I'm just wondering why you asked".

"I know and I get it. You're being cautious and you probably have no idea who to trust. But, you can trust me. I'm not like the rest of them. I do know that if my mom just died a few months ago, my dad was M.I.A and I got stuck with people like the Spencer's, 'ok' would be the farthest thing from what I'd be. Plus, I noticed you hiding your tears. Your mouth says one thing but your eyes say another." The tears just started falling.

"Uh un, honey. It's too many people around here that go to your aunt and uncles church and they report back everything they see. Suck those tears back up. Otherwise, you'll get in trouble again and here comes a group of them now." I did exactly what she said and put my smile back on.

"I used to be a member of their church until I got sense enough to leave. I'm an outcast now." "Hey Quetta! Who's your little friend?"

"This is Pastor Spencer's niece, Karen. She's helping me do my rounds."

"Um…. And she let her go with you? I wonder why".

"Surprising ain't it?" Quetta replied.

They stared at each other for a minute then we started walking again.

"What was that all about?" I asked.

"Let's just say I'm the black sheep of the church and my family and everybody knows it. That's cause no one knows the truth."

"Well what's the truth?"

"That'll be a conversation for another time, but I'll tell you this. You stop all that crying. In order for you to survive around these people you gone need to have a thicker skin. Here's my number. If you ever need me just call".

We continued to work in silence until we met back up with my aunt.

"So what have you ladies been up to?" she asked.

"Nothing much…just working. She was really well behaved but she is super quiet."

"Oh really I'm surprised. She's usually a little chatter box at home".

I shook my head but said nothing.

"Well, we have to get moving. Thanks for taking her off my hands for a while."

"No problem. I actually enjoyed her company even though she didn't say much. She can hang out with me anytime."

We left and headed back home. I was thankful for the quiet ride. As soon as we got to the house I went to my room and stayed there for several days. I sat in the corner of the room looking out the window each day, watching the sun rise and set. Staring at the oddly shaped clouds as they rolled by, listening to the leaves rustle as the wind whistled through the cracks of my window, I wondered what was going to happen next. Mapping out how I was going to get myself out this situation with no money was exhausting. On about the third day of me hiding in my room my aunt called me downstairs.

"We need to talk little girl. Have a seat." She commanded.

"Yes ma'am". I hung my head and did as I was told.

"Ain't no sense in hiding in that room. I still know you're there. You not gone be living in my house for free. You need to get a job so you can prepare yourself to get out. You want to be grown so I'm gone treat you like you grown. You gone pay me to stay here."

"Yes ma'am".

To me that sounded like a taste of freedom. I went upstairs got dressed and hit the streets. As I walked around the city I was attempting to come up with a plan. Day in and day out, I rose at the crack of dawn and dressed as quickly as possible. I wanted to be gone by the time everybody woke up to return as late in the evening as I could. I wasn't always looking for a job though. Sometimes I was just enjoying the freedom of being away from them. I didn't have a hustle or anything to fall back on. Planning how to get out from where I was but still have a roof over my head felt like trying to solve a foreign mystery written in a language I didn't speak. I was scared. Fear embedded itself in my soul and I tried to run from it daily. I was running from a fear that was stitched to my back, holding a plastic bag over my head, and smothering me. There was no escape. This was my reality.

While out one day I ran into Jacquetta and we started talking again. Meeting her became a ritual after that. I tried to talk to her as often as possible. She could relate to so many of my unspoken feelings even though I never revealed them. I wanted to know how. She was intriguing to me and I wanted to know more. Today we were meeting up at this cozy little coffee shop called *A Piece of Heaven,* on the upper east side. They played really good R&B slow jams. I loved sitting in their big brightly colored, high back, plush chairs that felt like they were hugging you as you sat in them. When I walked in she was already there.

"Hey little lady!" She greeted me with a smile and a hug. "How are you?"

"I'm here" I stated.

"How is everything going?" She inquired.

"The same. My aunt is telling me I have to pay her to stay there. So, I need a job. When I'm not actually looking for something or with you I'm at the church. I joined as many activities as I could think of just to stay away from the house to make it seem like I'm really trying to do something. So, here's my question to you…. Why are you the outcast just for leaving the church?"

"Wow! You went deep fast. You not gone ease your way into it?"

"Oh… I thought that was easy. My bad."

"No, it wasn't. Don't you want to talk about something else

though?"

"Sure. Once you answer my question" I replied with a smile.

She stared at me as if I had just said something that broke her heart. She took a deep breath, let out a big sigh then began.

"I'm the black sheep because my mother had an affair with your uncle which produced me. A few months before my 15th birthday I started acting out and misbehaving. I was only cutting up because my mom had a new boyfriend that she cherished more than me. I wanted her attention… She wanted her freedom! So rather than deal with me, she sent me to live with my father. Your aunt hated me from the moment I walked in the door. Every time she saw me I was a constant reminder to her that he cheated. She made sure to never let me forget it. Her name for me was Mattress Tier."

"Mattress Tier?"

"Yea, because she said I was no better than my mom was. That all my mom was ever good for was being on her back on somebody's mattress and laying on my back would be the only thing I'd ever be destined to do. It was inevitable. It was my destiny just like being a hoe was my mama's. I was born a mattress baby and I'd die a mattress whore. Some of the things that woman would come up with to say, only someone with pure wickedness could come up with. When he wasn't around she made me pay for what my mama did. I hated her and I didn't hide it when I should've." She let out another big sigh, shook her head, and got real quiet for a minute. I could tell it still bothered her. So, I sat quietly in hopes that she'd continue. Shortly after, she began again.

"People saw my reaction but they took a blind eye and deaf ear to the things she did. She was an angel… a saint…. and I was supposed to be grateful. The moments where she'd grab my skin and twist it or jab her elbow into my side or my face and pretend it was an accident were torture. The times she'd sneak up behind me going to wash clothes push me down the stairs and laugh, she'd lie and say I fell. She'd break a glass intentionally, creep up next to me and cut me with a piece of it. If my father asked what happened she'd tell him I broke another dish on purpose and cut myself in the process. She'd snicker then say that's what I got for always acting ugly. The list goes on and on." She paused again. Tears began to roll down her face as she reminisced. I passed her a napkin and waited on her to start up again.

"About four months into me living with them, I felt this heavy weight on me in the night. I woke up staring into my father's face. Confused, I struggled to get free. My arms and legs were tied to the bed frame. As I looked around the room I saw my nightgown was raised…. panties ripped apart on the floor.... MY FATHER in me. As I screamed he whispered "I love it when they put up a fight but no one is here to hear you. It's just us. Just relax baby girl… daddies got you." The tears ran faster down her face as she looked at me and asked, "Is any of this sounding familiar to you… 'dead sister's daughter'?" I sat there speechless. She continued. "The first moment I saw you standing there with her, fighting to hide the tears in your eyes, I knew he had already got you."

"Did you ever say anything?" I asked.

"Did you?" she questioned.

"Who do you tell when the majority of the city goes to the church and they're either in his bed or in his pockets? When I told my mother she let me come back to live with her but we never spoke of it again. Listen. Get away from them before they kill you."

She slowly stood up and walked out the door. It must be easier to lie to yourself than to tell someone the most horrific time in your life, knowing you have to face them after that. For weeks, I still went to the coffee shop and waited for her to show but she never did. I guess admitting the hurt was more than she could bear because watching her walk out the door was the last time I saw her.

Chapter 5

I began attending church more, thinking the more I was out of the house the better things would be. I attended every choir rehearsal, usher board meeting, bible study and youth group activity. I even assisted the children's ministry. I figured the only hard part about using the church as an escape would be that I had to encounter my uncle more. Honestly, I'd rather deal with him than my aunt because he wouldn't hurt me around large groups of people. In front of everyone he treated me like I mattered. My goal was to stay in front of people as much as possible in an attempt to have peace. That was short lived though because as soon as he realized I was hanging out at the church he began insisting on me riding with him. I refused but the more I refused the more pissed off my aunt became and the harder he insisted. So, I conceded in an attempt to tame the mounting tension. Nervously, I climbed in the truck each day, wondering how long these rides would last before he tried something. Needless to say the safe rides didn't remain safe.

On one of the trips he put his hand on my knee and began to rub up and down my leg. I didn't know it then but this was the first of many rides that all played out the same. The first few times I tensed up but after about a month I got used to it. I'd brace myself for what was to come and accept it.

"I've been missing you and our time together. I love the way you make me feel."

I slowly turned my head to look at him then back out the window. "So tell me… inquiring minds want to know. How does abusing children make you feel?"

"Baby girl… I'm not abusing you. I'm helping you. I'm teaching you. Everything I do to you is biblical. All throughout the book of Genesis and Exodus relatives was sleeping with each other. Hell, Amram married his daddy's sister! That's how Moses came about and over in Romans 12:10 it talks about being kind and affectionate to one another. I'm just doing my part. I want to make sure you learn everything you need to know in life and at the same time I'm welcoming you into your womanhood. I'm teaching you key things you'll need to know in order to please your man. See, as Christians we have a twofold ministry. I'm making sure my ministry touches you on the inside and out."

"Who said I'm going to have a man to please? I'm gay."

"Well hell a woman too! But if you are gay can I join in? I'm sure I can teach both of you a thing or two."

I looked at him out the corner of my eye, rolled my eyes, and stared back out the window. I didn't say anything else. He kept talking but I tuned him out till I felt his hand begin to pull my legs apart. I pushed his hand away which really pissed him off. He grabbed me by my hair, pushed my head into the window, and yelled "This gone be the last muthafucking time your little ungrateful ass is gone reject me!" He snatched the truck to the side of the road a few miles from the church then grabbed my legs and pulled them apart. I punch him, trying to push him off me. He pushed my head into the window even harder. The glass cracked and blood started steaming down my face. God, help me. I'm so sick of this. Just then a car pulled up behind us. From behind they could see us fighting. It was Deacon Ryan and Sister Stephanie. Deacon Ryan blew his horn and got out of his car to walk up to the truck.

"Good evening Pastor, is everything alright?"

"Yes sir. I'm just having a little disagreement with my niece here."

"You need any help?"

"Naw, I'm good. Thank you for asking. We're heading right down here to the church now."

As they talked I sat up in the seat, adjusted my clothes, and stared out the window.

"Ok. I'll see you there" he said and walked back to the car.

My uncle looked at me and said, "straighten up, fix yo face and know that this ain't over."

When we arrived at the church I ran inside and down the steps to the bathroom. I reached for the paper towels, wet them and wiped the blood from my face. When I heard footsteps, I thought it was him coming to finish what he started and I froze. I let out a soft sigh of relief when I noticed it was just Sister Stephanie coming in the door.

"So, you wanna tell me what the hell was going on out there?"

I didn't say anything. I just looked at her and continued to clean myself up.

"What happened to your face?"

"It was an accident." I knew better than to say anything to anybody. I knew what my life was already like daily. I could only imagine what would happen if I opened my mouth.

"What happened to the window of the truck?"

"Something hit it."

"Is there somewhere else you can go?"

"No"

"Question…"

"Possible answer…"

"Are they hurting you?"

I didn't respond. A tear fell and I wiped it quickly. Once I got my face cleaned up I started fixing my clothes and hair.

"Does your aunt know what's going on?"

As I looked up at her in the mirror my eyes filled with tears. I took a deep breath attempting to keep them from falling but a few fell anyway. I hung my head, took another deep breath, wiped my face once again then continued trying to pull myself together.

"And she's not doing anything to stop him? Is she helping him?"

Again, I looked at her, looked away and continued doing what I was doing.

Tears began to roll down her face.

"Don't cry for me. Crying's not allowed"

"Who told you some shit like that?"

She placed her hand on my cheek. I pressed my face into the palm of her hand as tears dripped from my eyes onto her fingers. The sweet smell of her fingers, the gentleness and warmth of her touch, my mama use to touch my face like this, for a moment I lost myself in the feeling of the affection and felt as if everything was going to be alright again. She grabbed me and hugged me as we cried together. I didn't know how much time I had but my heart wished this moment could last forever. As hard as I fought to swallow my tears I couldn't stop them from falling. My tears and silence told her everything she needed to know. When we heard someone coming she ran to a stall and straightened her face. I grabbed more paper towels and wiped mine. It was my uncle.

"Hey sexy little lady…. You ready to finish where we left off?"

I looked at him and glanced toward the stall but didn't say anything. He grabbed me and turned me towards him.

"Stop!"

"Oh, you still playing that hard to get shit? You ain't learned your lesson by now?"

"Stop! Get off me! Please stop." At this point tears are streaming down my face even harder now. "Why do you keep doing this? Let me go."

I pulled away. He pushed me into the counter and ripped my pants open and started kissing my neck. One hand pulled at my panties while forcing my hand down his pants with his other hand. He heard a noise that stopped him. Sister Stephanie was moving the tissue roll. She flushed the toilet and walked out of the stall. He stepped back. I moved to the side and began fixing my clothes again.

"Hello Pastor…"

"Why, hello Sister Stephanie. How are you on this fine evening?"

"Good and yourself?"

"I'm doing great" he said as he adjusted his clothes and walked out.

"He's raping you?" she squealed

"No, he's just ministering to me"

"Ministering to you?"

"You should check out Judges 19 even the bible called it rape"

"Has anyone ever talked to you about sex before?"

"No"

Silence fell as she handed me a rubber band and showed me how to fix my pants so no one could tell the button was missing. We walked out of the bathroom. As we were moving passed the door my uncle went to Deacon Ryan and whispered.

"Hey man, yo girl saw something she ain't have no business. I need you to get her in line and make sure she don't open her damn mouth to nobody."

"No problem man. I gotchu."

Deacon Ryan walked over to where Sister Stephanie and I were grabbed her, slapped her to the ground, and said "You need to learn how to keep yo fucking nose out of other people's business".

"What are you talking about? I didn't do anything" she says as she's getting up off the floor.

"You know exactly what the fuck I'm talking about and you bet not open yo mouth to say shit!" He punches her in the face she hits the floor again. This time she's out cold. He turned to me "and you bet not open yo fucking mouth either or you'll be next."

I just stood there looking at him. I glanced over at my uncle. He smiled

"See baby girl, it don't come no bigger than me." Deacon Ryan walked over to him and said, "Man you ain't got to worry about nothing."

"I appreciate that" he replied.

They shook hands and walked upstairs. I waited till the coast was clear and helped Sister Stephanie up off the floor. She looked at me with tears pouring from her eyes. She didn't say a word. She just walked away. During bible study I couldn't help but to stare at her. She wouldn't even look in my direction. Once church was over I walked up to her, took her hand and told her I was sorry. She dropped her head and walked away. She never spoke to me again and I understood.

Chapter 6

The next day was choir rehearsal. Minister Audrey Jackson was our director. She was the most hilarious person and biggest gossip I had ever met. She knew everybody's business and had no problem telling it. She told me everything about everybody, including myself. She loved seeing me coming too so she could tell me the latest and I loved going early so I could have more time to laugh at her. As soon as I hit the door she came flying out the sanctuary

"Hey demon seed I heard you been causing quite the stir around your parts…"

"I have? Do share…"

"Yea, you have… you didn't know?"

"Girl naw tell me! What I do?"

"I heard you done took over the house, threatened ya auntie, don't clean up behind yourself, and why didn't you tell me you had a new boyfriend?"

"I do? Well who is he?

"Why you playing like all this is new to you? Hell, I don't know who he is but apparently ya ass is too hot to trot and you on the verge of getting put out cause ya auntie walked in and caught ya'll having sex on the kitchen counter."

"WOOOOOOW REALLY??? Boooooooooy if walls could talk and truths got told we'd all bust hell wide open!!! Anyway, you got a note for me to take to the office?"

She was secretly in love with my uncle so she would always send me to his office with messages for him that she wrote on little pieces of paper. She was also in love with Pastor Edwards, which was the Pastor at Greater Mount Mary M.B.C and my uncle's best friend. Pastor Edwards' church was up the block and around the corner from ours. The first thing I learned being in the church was that no matter what I saw, to keep my mouth shut. Hanging around so many leaders in the church I saw a whole lot but didn't say a word. Minister Jackson was a character unlike any other though. She believed that she was destined to be a first lady and she was going to be one by any means necessary. If that meant she had to move someone out of their current position then so be it!

She did everything she could think of to get my uncle's attention. One Sunday, she wore this short tight-fitted, red mini dress and directed the choir. Now, Minister Jackson was a high yellow, red bone with dusty red hair. She was 5'2, 46 DD in the chest, had a flat stomach and was a size 12 in the waist. With a butt that looked like someone stuck two perfectly positioned basketballs under her dress, she always commanded attention. I didn't sing that day so I caught a good view of everything from where I sat. Every time she bounced up and down I could see the bottom of her butt cheeks. It didn't matter if the music was fast or slow. Anytime her back was to the congregation she made sure she was bouncing. The grin on my uncle's face told me he loved every bit of it. My aunt was so pissed! "You need to have a talk with her NOW!" She yelled at him as she stormed out the church.

We had two services that day. Just before the service ended, I noticed my uncle and Minister Jackson had both disappeared. Once service was over, Deacon Lang asked me to go find my uncle and tell him they had a situation that required his immediate attention. So, I went looking for him. I walked into his office only to discover Minister Jackson bent over his desk with her dress up. They were getting it in.

"Yes Jesus! Yes God!" She kept saying over and over again. I stood there with my mouth hanging open in shock by what I was seeing.

"Hurry up and get in here and close the door!" He screamed at me.

I gave him the message then quickly closed the door. I ran as fast as I could away from his office. As I ran away I thought to myself… WOW! That was all it took for her to get what she wanted? I shook my head, not paying attention to where I was walking, so I walked right into Deacon Lang.

"I'm sorry I wasn't paying attention to where I was going. I gave my uncle your message but he was taking care of another urgent matter. He'll be over as soon as he finishes."

In the meantime, my uncle sent Deacon Ryan over to talk to me.

"What did you see today?" Deacon Ryan asked.

"When? What are you talking about?" I pretended to be confused.

"What happened between your uncle and Minister Jackson?"

"Huh? Something happened between the two of them? What happened?"

He had the most dumbfounded look on his face. I guess my uncle didn't tell him the whole story before he sent him over to me, but I knew better than to open my mouth. He went back to my uncle they talked for a minute then they both walked over to me.

"Tell Deacon Ryan what happened when you walked in my office earlier." With a straight face and blank stare, I tilted my headed slightly to the side, scrunched up my nose and replied.

"Tell him what? I gave you the message Deacon Lang told

me to tell you. Then I left and told Deacon Lang you were taking care of another urgent matter and you'd be over as soon as you finished."

He smiled "My girl... That's my baby girl! That's what I'm talking about!" He patted me on my back and walked off grinning from ear to ear. I knew it was a test and I knew the consequences behind failing it too. From that moment on I became the secret keeper, the person who had to run interference, the errand girl, and everyone's favorite.

Chapter 7

Shortly after that I managed to land my first job making $10.00 an hour at Fairview Park which was the fairgrounds just outside downtown, on the lakefront. It's where all the festivals happened. Fairview celebrated everything from each individual nationality to festivals for every season. In between those they had festivals just because someone wanted to have one. I tried to work them all too! I was on the grounds crew. My job was to clean up during and after all the festivals. I hated the job because I didn't like cleaning up after people all day long. My feet always hurt to the point of burning. I couldn't stand being outdoors but I liked making money. Money was my path to freedom so I didn't care how much I hated my job. I sucked it up and went every day, all day. I needed that check to get free!

When I got my first paycheck I opened a student bank account at First National Bank. All I needed was a student ID and it didn't require a parent or guardian's signature. I was super excited! This account meant that nobody besides me would know how much money I had. I was the only one with access to it. I set up my paychecks to go direct deposit and for my bank statements to be sent electronically. There would be no trace of my account anywhere. I'd always tell my aunt that I made less than what it actually was so she wouldn't try to take my entire check. Then I'd give her what she thought was half and save the rest so I could move out. My goal was to work as many hours as possible each week so I could save quicker. I prayed people would call in so they would need me to stay late. If I stayed late it was overtime that put me one step closer to my goal. If there was something going on I needed to be there.

Of all the festivals I worked that year Pride Fest was the worst! I thought my day was going to be easy because I was assigned to clean the children's area, the bathrooms near there, all the shops out front and the Budweiser stage area… where the concerts were held. There were no children at this festival so my assignment would be light duty. I'd be able to relax and chill all day. I arrived early at 7 a.m. while the grounds were quiet and empty. The wind blew just enough to push small pieces of garbage across the concrete as I walked by. Most people called in because they hated this festival. I didn't care. That meant more money for me. I was saving up for my freedom run… hell I needed all the money I could get. I was ready to close the place down! I was just thinking about how big my check would be working open to close for this festival.

When we first walked out to the fairgrounds everybody was just cleaning everywhere in preparation of the gates to open before we went to our assigned areas. I got in and started cleaning. Everything was perfect! The sun was shining, but it wasn't too hot and there was a beautiful breeze coming in off the lake.

"We're about to have a quick meeting. I need everybody to meet me in front of the Children's theater stage." Jim our manager announced. We all ran over to see what was going on.

"I have a brief announcement since we have so many call ins today we want to know how many of you are willing to cover multiple areas. Those of you who volunteer will not only get paid overtime but we will give you double pay for working all day and covering multiple areas. It's not mandatory but if you would like to volunteer please raise your hand." I was the first one to throw my hand in the air.

However, I had no clue of what I was up against.

I didn't know that at Pride Fest everything goes. It was like one big orgy of church folks! Everything I didn't see at church I saw working this festival. The gates opened at 10 a.m. and by noon the place was packed. Vendors had set up their shops. I had never seen such an array of rainbows, gay pride merchandise and sex toys! As I cleaned, I looked around at each vendor table. My curiosity was piqued about many of the items being displayed. I listened to the conversations and laughed at a lot of the things people said. They felt free to be themselves and there was no holding anything back. I strolled along trying to complete the area I was in so I could head over to where I was originally stationed. I began to see people from every church I'd ever been to. All their secrets came out with them. Everybody was kissing and screwing everybody else! Brother Carl, who was head of the usher board at our church, and Brother John, who was head of the usher board at Greater Mount Mary M.B.C, walked up on me dressed as women!

"I can expect that I'll have no trouble out of you little girl…" speechless I scanned Carl from head to toe

"Uh…Hellllllllo!" he waved his hand in front of my face

"What in the Plum D Hell?" I replied

"Well, don't stand there with yo mouth open honey. Something just might get stuck in there. This is my life outside of that hell hole of a church we go to. Baby, I'm a queen and I'm fierce with my shit! I bet you wish you looked half as good as I do, don't you?"

"You got boobs…but DAMN ya'll look good! I have to give it to you. You did that! You really did the damn thang on that one."

"Why thank you!"

"But keep it between us cause I like MY Business to stay just that way… MINE!"

"I don't know what you're talking about. I see nothing… I know nothing."

"Oh, ok then. Good! As long as you know… Cause I didn't want to have to whoop yo lil ass and risk breaking a nail."

I laughed "You couldn't whoop my ass in a dream even if your life depended on it. Let alone reality!"

"Oh my… look Bae! Little miss tin man tryna have some hort! It's about time you start standing up for yourself instead of being everybody's puppet."

"I'm not a puppet. I just do what I gotta do to stay safe. At the end of the day I still need a place to rest my head"

"Real Talk!"

I bowed my head farewell and proceeded on to my area. I must admit I almost didn't recognize them. They looked so good. Better than most of the women I'd seen. If I didn't know them I would've thought they were actually women!

As I entered into the children's area I walked right into Sister Courtney, who was over the children's ministry, and Chasity, her assistant. They were having sex on one of the slides in the playground! "Uh… excuse me. You can't do that here." They were so caught up in the moment that they hadn't heard nor seen me walk over. I shook my head then tapped her on the shoulder and repeated myself.

"Uh… excuse me. You can't do that here." She jumped because I startled her.

"You can't do that here" I said again.

"OH, Shit! I didn't know you worked here!"

"SHIT! I didn't know you liked girls either so I guess we

both just learned something knew about each other huh?"

"Damn, you interrupting my flow" Chasity said as she began standing up wiping her mouth.

"I don't give a fuck Bitch this right here ain't ya bedroom!"

"BITCH! Who the fuck you…" She stopped mid-sentence as she looked up and saw it was me.

"OMG KAREN!"

"Are ya'll fucking kiddin' me? LIKE SERIOUSLY!!!!! YOU'RE the one dipped down between her legs and shit! When the hell did ya'll start liking chicks?" I was surprised and pissed. You bitches be the main ones bashing gay people and low and behold both you muthafukas gay! You hypocritical bitches!!! You know what let me stay in my lane. But, here." I handed them my towel and my spray bottle of bleach. "Wipe all ya twat juices off my damn slide and get ya ass out my area."

"Don't be mad. Just let me show you what I can do. I promise you'll like it."

"Girl Get Cha Ass!!!"

"I bet I can turn you out!"

"Naw not Miss I can't stand gay people! It's an abomination… All them hoes going to hell."

I took my cleaning supplies back and walked past them as if I didn't know who they were. It's crazy! I see and talk to these people all the time yet never knew how many of them were leading double lives. I left them and stumbled right into Sister Mary and Minister Paula on the other side of the playground having sex. My mouth dropped, my stomach turned, and my heart sank. The two women I respected the most was just as hypocritical as everyone else preaching against the very thing they doing.

"Damn I see why nobody wanted to work today. Not ya'll

too!"

"Karen, listen honey we can explain"

"Listen to what!!! What chu gon' explain? How you like twat or how your not really gay you just like getting' ya twat ate? What chu gon' explain to me? Is the whole damn church on the downlow? Cause I done seen damn near all ya'll out here screwing each other!"

"Karen baby listen…"

"I looked up to ya'll! Respected ya'll! And you out here creepin' like the ones you talk about too. Ya'll ain't shit! By the way don't walk into ya husbands they're out here too!" I walked off.

I wanted them to feel the same hurt I did. This was too much sex for me. I felt like I was walking through a live porn filming! I tried to quickly run away from my area only to run into Minister Calvin bent over on the park bench with Pastor Kendall doing him from behind! I learned so much about sex that day. It completly changed the way I looked at all of them. From then on I didn't put anything past anybody because none of them were as they appeared to be.

The reality had set in that all of these people were the most saved people I knew, and I began to wonder if this was what knowing Jesus was all about. I radioed for my boss and told him I was heading in for my first break. I felt so filthy. As I was heading toward one of our break rooms, I saw Derrick, the boy I was dating at the time. Markus and I had only been separated for about 3 weeks when Derrick and I started dating. Neither of us liked the long-distance relationship and just stopped talking. When I met Derrick I just let him occupy what little time I did have. Derrick and I had been dating for six months so I was astonished to see him at a festival like this. When he saw me he tried to run but it was too late. I had already seen him kissing Anthony, which was my home girl Stacy's boyfriend.

"Hey baby, I thought you weren't working today." He reached to hug me. I pushed him away.

"Nigga get ya punk ass out my fucking face! Why would I not be working and you know I'm on a fucking paper chase? Then you gon' come at me like you didn't know I saw you with this muthafucka! You know what I'm done! I CAN'T! I WON'T! I'M DONE! I JUST CAN'T!" I threw my hands in the air, walked past them, went to the break room, put my head down and cried. My chest felt like somebody kicked me in it, it became hard to breath. I couldn't believe my eyes but to really react would cause me to lose my job. I desperately needed my job. As I walked by I kept telling myself my freedom was more important than their secrets… so don't react. I remember thinking to myself… I can't trust anybody. I have got to get away from these people if it's the last thing I do.

I needed God to help me tell Stacy because she was head over hills in love with Anthony. They had been dating for three years and he had just proposed to her a week ago. Now, Stacy was four years older than I was and super spiritual. We used to talk all the time but due to our work schedules we hadn't had time to catch up. This was not a conversation we could have via text message or over the phone. So, the next day I texted her to tell her I needed to talk to her and that it was really important. We had one of the best choirs in the city so we planned to meet up on Tuesday to talk before the choir meeting. The meeting was to discuss whether or not we would be allowed to go on tour and to get the new rehearsal schedule. The choir was made up of a variety of young ministers, deacons in training and regular young people. When I saw Stacy I headed her way. She looked pissed.

"Hey girl… what's wrong?"

"Give me a second. I need to handle some business before we talk."

She marched into the sanctuary where everybody had already begun gathering. When she pushed the doors open they slammed against the wall, which startled the room and got everyone's attention. A silence fell as we stared at her, waiting to see what was about to happen. She proceeded down the center aisle towards Anthony. She jumped in his face and asked, "Are you cheating?"

"No baby! I'm not cheating." He looked at me and I had the most shocked look on my face. He looked back toward her. "Why you keep looking at her? You sleeping with her?"

With my face scrunched up I yelled "HEEEELL NAW!!! IT AIN'T ME!"

"Baby, I don't know what you're talking about. I'm not cheating on you" he said.

"You're lying..." Her voice elevated just slightly.

"No, I'm not. I would never cheat on you."

"YES, YOU ARE BECAUSE I FELT IT" she screams with tears pouring from her eyes!

"I FELT HIM IN YOU! DO YOU KNOW WHAT IT FEELS LIKE TO WAKE UP OUT OF YOUR SLEEP TO SOMEONE FUCKING YOU IN YOUR ASS AND YOU NOT ENJOYING IT!!!!!!! I FELT YOU CHEATING!"

"So... who is he? Who is the nigga you're cheating on me with?"

"Baby... I'm sorry. I...." Before he could get it out she slaps him.

"I don't want your Damn 'Baby I'm sorry's'! I want to know who the fuck you cheating on me with. What nigga is better than me?"

"We were all sleeping with each other. Me and Derrick were together, Tyson and Kevin, Charles and Broderick. I just tried it. I didn't know I was gon' like it. I'm sorry. I didn't mean for you to find out like this. I'm sorry I lied to you."

Anthony and Derrick were both ministers. The rest of the guys he named were either deacons, armor bearers, ministry leaders or filled multiple roles in the church. He dropped his head. Everyone else's eyes got big however the room remained quiet. She wasn't the only one with tears falling from her eyes. There were six of us who hung out together regularly and he just confessed that all of our boyfriends were sleeping with each other! Stacy stormed out and I followed behind her. I think we all needed time to process what had just happened. I heard a roar of laughter erupt as I walked out the door. It seemed like life was throwing stinging blows at me every chance it got. I didn't realize my aunt and uncle were sitting there listening to everything. My aunt came out to where we were and spoke to me in her usual fashion.

"Little girl... shit happens to the best of us so wipe your face, suck it up and keep it moving!"

"Yes ma'am" I replied as I wiped my face. Yet again I swallowed tears that had a right to be shed. I thought I was in love and even though it felt like my heart was broken into a million tiny pieces, I choked and stuffed my emotions down till I was numb inside. I went on as if nothing happened. Stacy and I looked at each other. She shook her head and started to leave.

"Hey! Where you goin'?"

"I'm getting outta here. I can't play this role no more. They win."

"I wish it was that easy for me."

"It is. Just leave... You ain't nothing but a sex toy. Do you really think they gone come looking for you?" That was the last time Stacy stepped foot in our church.

Chapter 8

For weeks her words kept echoing in my head. Every so often we'd talk or run into each other. Each time we did she'd ask… 'so you ready to break free yet?' And each time I normally wouldn't respond. She'd say 'oh ok then'. Then she'd change the subject but this time I said 'yes'.

We started planning my escape almost immediately. I was worried that they would be able to follow me from school since I hadn't quite finished yet. When I went to school on Monday I met with my guidance counselor. Her name was Mrs. Tracy Brooks. I told her I had an emergency and I needed her help. I made her pinky swear she'd never tell anyone. Although I knew that legally she was required to report it, I prayed God would help her see that it was in *our* best interest for her to keep her mouth closed. I told her everything that was happening in my life from the beginning. About how my life had become full of everyone else's secrets as if my own weren't enough.

She started crying and explained that by law she is required to report it. My heart dropped. I could feel it beating in the pit of my stomach. As she reached for her phone I jumped to my feet and grabbed it before she could. I started to panic and quickly explained to her who my aunt and uncle were. I needed to make her understand why she couldn't say anything and what happened to the last person that tried to help me. She had to know how many people in top notch positions my uncle had in his pocket that were willing destroy the life of someone else to protect his secrets. If she told anybody they would kill her long before the authorities could find me to try to help.

Also, my uncle was best friends with half the police force and they all attended our church. The likelihood of her finding someone that wasn't corrupt was slim to none. I went on to explain what I was planning to do. I needed her to keep my secret not just for her safety but for mine too. So, she did. She didn't know who to trust just like I didn't. When she agreed to help me she reached out to hug me but the way her hands moved I guess I thought she was going to hit me or something. I jumped back.

"It's alright baby" and held me for the longest time. We cried together for what seemed like hours. As she rubbed my back "let it out… it's ok… I'm sure this cry is long overdue."

I replied "I can't. I have to suck it up. I'm not allowed to cry because life happens to everybody."

"Yes, you can. You're safe here."

"Yea, but when I leave here I have to go back into my reality. I can't let myself go for a second so let's just get this over with." I began wiping my face as I pulled myself back together.

"Ok sweetie. Let me pull up your whole file and take a look at it."

You could tell she wanted to keep talking but she didn't. She did as I asked. As she looked through my file she discovered that I could actually graduate early. Technically, I only needed two more classes. See, the school I was originally in back home was for the gifted and talented. All my classes were Advanced Placement (AP) classes. One of my regular classes equaled two of their normal ones. I really didn't need any of the credits I had in my current schedule. They were just filler courses. Instead, she entered me into a work study program where I would work part time in the administration office. This was awesome because it paid $8.00 an hour. I got paid weekly too. I was also still working at Fairview getting paid every two weeks. I tried to keep as much of that check as I could to have as a cushion when I left. Freedom was looking closer and closer by the minute! I worked during the mornings in the admin office, went to the two classes I needed to graduate, then headed to work at the festival grounds in the evening.

Stacy was excited when I told her this was my last semester in school. I'd be finished in December! I didn't care about walking across the stage. I had no one who cared enough to come see me anyway. I just wanted to get done so when I left I wouldn't be able to be tracked. I told them to mail my diploma to Stacy's P.O. Box. She had just moved into a nice two-bedroom apartment in the Suburbs of Lexington, KY which was about an hour and 20 minutes from where we were. Since no one knew we were still talking to each other it was easy for us to plan the escape. I didn't know anything about being out on my own, but I knew whatever it entailed had to be a whole lot better than my life at that moment. I was ready for it.

In the meantime, I still played my role pretending like everything was okay even though the church had gotten incredibly worse. Since everyone knew that no matter what they did I would keep my mouth closed, I had all kinds of friends that did everything under the sun. I got invited to all the parties, all the outings, and sometimes I even got paid to keep people company. For the first time since my mama passed away, I felt like I belonged somewhere and I wasn't alone anymore. I started spending the night a lot at Sister Mary's house. She had two daughters, Shannon and Kayla. She added me in as her third child. We were known as the three musketeers because when I wasn't working we were all together. She was another one of my uncle's mistresses but she was also my aunt's best friend so they let me go over as often as possible. I felt free. I felt like belonging was slowly filling the parts of me that were empty. Even when her girls were gone, Mary and I would just hang out on my off days.

One day, the two of us were just hanging out watching a movie. After a while she got up, walked towards the back of the house and disappeared. I thought she had gone to the bathroom or to get more snacks. After so long of her not returning, I went to look for her. I searched high and low but couldn't find her anywhere. I noticed a door that I had never really paid any attention to before. I only spotted it this time because it was slightly open. When I opened it I heard music playing. I walked up the stairs and into this room covered in plants. It reminded me of like a indoor greenhouse but it smelled funny. I saw Mama Mary on the other side of the room trimming one of the plants. I headed towards her.

"What are you doing? You left me."

"Oh, is the movie over already?"

"Almost, but you were gone so long I came to see if you were ok."

"Yea I'm good. I got up because somebody needed to place an order."

"An order for what? What are these plants and why do they stink?"

"It's ganja baby. These here are home grown Weed plants. This that real shit right here! These them real money makers right here!" I learned all about weed and its different types at all the parties I was going to. Most of them told me she was their supplier so I wasn't at all surprised by what I saw even though I pretended to be.

"And you're growing it? Damn Ma!"

I walked back downstairs in disbelief. When the girls came home she called us all into the kitchen for a talk.

"Listen, all of you are old enough now to where we can talk about some for real shit. I need to have a grown woman conversation with ya'll. So, cop a squat and listen up cause I ain't gone repeat myself."

We all sat down around the kitchen counter. We watched as she poured each of us a drink. I tasted it.

"What is this?"

"That's some grown woman shit right there. It's Absolute and cranberry juice. Drink up while we talk. You gone need it."

"Um ok" I replied.

"If you don't remember nothing else in life remember this… One of the most important things you'll ever need to learn in life is that everybody needs a side hustle."

"Well what's your side hustle Mama?" Shannon asked.

"Yea" Kayla chimed in.

"I'm a jack of all trades but a master of none."

"What does that even mean?" I asked.

She laughed "It means I have my hand in a little bit of everything. I'm a spiritual street pharmacist… hell, sometimes a counselor even. I can take people to places in heaven that Jesus won't even let them get to."

"How do you do that?" I asked.

"Easy! I aid the sick wherever the spirit leads me." She started jumping up and down, jerking her body around like she was shouting.

"Hallelujah…Hallelujah….AYE! God loves a cheerful giver. I provide them with a spiritual supplement that helps temporarily strengthen their mind and body while soothing their soul. So… you want to start making some real money or what?"

"Of Course!"

"Absolutely!"

"Yeah!"

"Ok, but you must know something else that's important…

1. Always keep yo mouth shut. When you hustlin' people gone always try to get you caught up in some shit. Don't fall for it.

2. If you ever get caught by the police, say NOTHING. No matter what they threaten you with. Since all of you are minors if you do get in trouble it'll only be a slap on the wrist.

3. DON'T GET YO ASS CAUGHT!!!!!!! Got it?"

"Yes Ma'am" we replied in unison.

"Good. Cause for some of the shit I do, my kitchen just ain't big enough. So, I use the one at the church since that's where most of my clients are anyway. Now, from now on ya'll are gone be my movers and shakers. Finish up those drinks. I'll be right back."

She went and got a chart and came back and told us all to gather around. She explained to us the different types of drugs there were and what they do to you. She taught us how strong and addictive each one was, which ones were okay for us to try and which ones we should never try. By the end of the day we could look at different items and tell by the way it was shaped, looked or smelled, or by the color exactly what kind of drug it was. We could even identify what the ounces or grams measured out into. We also learned how to properly hand it to someone without it being a noticeable exchange. We were pros by the end of the night. The next evening, we headed to choir rehearsal. That's when I learned how to make crack for the first time. We did it in the basement of the church. When you walked through the kitchen there was this poorly lit, long hallway that extended off from it. At the end of that hall there was another room. It was a slightly smaller, darker version of the main kitchen. I mean… hey, why not? Everything else was going on around here.

Chapter 9

After choir rehearsal Shannon, Kayla, and I were hanging out in the basement, waiting on the adults to get out of a meeting so we could go home. Mama Mary was in the kitchen cooking. The closer I got to it the stench became more and more putrid, unlike anything I had every smelled in my life! My stomach felt like it was doing summer salts from the smell. If I had to describe the scent I guess I would say it was kinda like burnt plastic mixed with urine and something else. I kept walking towards it because I was curious about what she was doing.

"What is that smell?" I asked.

"Here… put a mask on, cut the fan up, and close the door. It's the supplements."

"A supplement of what?"

"Remember when I was talking to you about crack?"

"Like what's on the ground?" We both laughed.

"No fool! Last night…"

"Sorry, airhead moment. Oh Yea, ok I remember."

"Well come here and let me show you how to make it."

She took me step-by-step through the process of how to make and break down crack. While learning the process, I understood the purpose of wearing a mask. As I was being mentored by her I also became her main "candy girl". I quit working at Fairview as soon as I became a candy girl because it paid four, sometimes five times more money than what I could collect in two weeks cleaning the fair grounds. My first time making a drop I was super nervous, but trying not to let it show. We were taught to never let your emotions get the best of you, you must control them at all times. Never allow your fear to show and when in trouble never let your opponent see you sweat. So, that's exactly what I did!

I didn't let my emotions or fear get the best of me. We were thrown to the wolves to sink or swim and I was determined to swim at all costs. I kept practicing different signals, hand offs, and working on my speed running to and from destinations until I was able to master it. The money was super-fast and good! Shit, great even on most days. I was on a straight paper chase! I didn't have time to care where it came from. I needed it! The feel and control of so much paper running through my fingers at any given moment was a thrill to me. I've never seen so much cash! I also learned quickly to watch how much money I was depositing into my bank account at one time.

The church folks were our biggest clients especially when we had anniversaries, revivals and other events. I mean ALL the church folks, including my uncle. The best thing about it all was my aunt didn't know about the money so I didn't have to share. I gave her what I wanted her to have. She never knew I left Fairview. No one told her. The people that knew kept my secret like I kept theirs. I dropped down to only giving her about a hundred dollars every two weeks. I told her Fairview had cut my hours so I was volunteering more at the church.

I looked forward to occasions where all the community churches would gather at our church. To let me know they needed "candy" they would flag me over or send an usher to come get me. They'd rest their hand on my back or tug at my shirt. My reply would be "What chu need rocks or dust, green or pills?" You name it I had access to it. When they replied, I would get the candy in a bible, bulletin, or hand it to them with the church fan. If they ordered something on a larger scale I would hand them my purse or bookbag and ask them to hold on to my bag for me.

When service let out there was always a dinner in the basement of the church. That's where I did the most running. From table to table, minister to deacon, police officer to nurse, leaders to pastor, across the room I went. Leadership paid well most of them even tipped. On any given day, I could rake in a good five to six hundred dollars easy, if not more. I made more money in church than I did hanging around in the streets because everybody needed something different. Our motto was that *'we were there to supply ALL their spiritual needs…in the name of Jesus'*. I made sure everyone's needs were always met. I learned how to serve and how to serve well. I was slick about how I handed them what they needed too. I could slip something to someone and you would never even see my hands move. This is why I didn't know that Jesus was not just another nigga on the street selling a temporary fix!

There was another church across the street, down the street, and two blocks over. On Sundays, instead of being in service, I would spend it running from one church to another. Every time a new order came in I went running, literally running. I was the fastest runner Mama Mary had. I knew the more deliveries I made the more money I got. So, I always competed against myself to increase my time. I got paid almost double for going to the other churches in the neighborhood and because I could get in and out so quickly, plus I always got a tip. I think some of them only tipped so well because they wanted to make sure I kept my mouth shut but I was going to do that anyway. I knew what happened when you opened your mouth about other people's business.

One time, Sandy told Deacon Willard's wife about his habits. His wife confronted him and the wife threatened to divorce him if he didn't quit. Mama Mary paid a group of kids to beat Sandy up. They beat her within inches of her life and caused her to go blind in her left eye. She made everybody else stand there watching to make sure we knew if we opened our mouths we'd be next. Another time, I watched as she had some of the runners hold someone down while she injected them with drugs. She told their mama she caught them getting high. The church was never our safe haven. It was just our stomping grounds. These people were ruthless but claimed they did it all out of love. My life was already a living hell that I wasn't trying to make any worse. I did as I was directed nothing more nothing less.

Who was I gone tell anyway? Hell, the majority of the police department went to our church and most of them were clients too! It was very little happening I didn't know about yet said not a word. Fear kept my eyes blind and my lips sealed. All the adults talked to me about their problems. I was always giving someone advice on a situation or telling them how to handle a problem. I wanted so bad to help some of them understand why their life was hell. I wanted to tell what I knew that they didn't. The stuff that was really going on in their home and behind their back, but I couldn't. Instead, I advised them based off only the information they already knew. I was a dealer and a counselor all at the same time. Now I understood why Mama Mary said she nurtured their spirits. Our jobs were always two-fold.

During that same time, I was also hanging out with Mary's sister Ashley, who was one of the associate ministers at the church. She was also a former exotic dancer. Her stage name was "Sweetness". She used to tell us all about her past life and the types of clubs she worked in. The private parties she did and the quick cash she collected was amazing! She said those were her glory days, but she had to keep her body right because if she ever fell on hard times again, it would also be her fall back plan. She suggested that every woman needs a fall back plan.

It was the highest paying job she ever had. Ashley gave us all nicknames. We were Cinnamon, Sparkles and

Dimples. I was Dimples. I liked Ashley because she was such an open book about where she came from, where she aspired to be, and her plans to get there. She dreamed big and was always looking for the next big payout. Since so many of the men in the church complemented us on our body structures, she decided we should start charging them to look at it. Things started out with us just role playing. It was funny. A lot of the time she would act like the men in the church using their lines as she walked by us.

She would walk by swinging her left arm holding her dick, sit in a chair with her legs open and say

"Ummm… um… say lil mama why don't you come give big daddy a lap dance. I got some bills wit cha name on it".

Or she would walk up on you real close to where you could feel her breath on your neck and say

"Damn baby you turning me on! What do you say to dancing with me privately when you finish. I got a little friend that needs your attention".

For some of the girls they felt embarrassed and ashamed but Ashley convinced them it was ok. She would have long talks with them about blocking out what people said and focusing on the music. None of it bothered me though because the degrading comments couldn't make me feel any worse than my uncle did. I just shut it all out and forced my mind to go somewhere else like I did with him.

Once we mastered getting use to the demeaning comments, pats on our butt, and squeezes on our breasts we went to the church to learn a new trade. In the basement of the church there were 3 slender poles that stood underneath the main sanctuary. We trained on them daily. We learned how to utilize our stomach muscles and upper body strength to support our weight as we swung around the pole then held our positions. We were taught to do sexually suggestive moves on and around the pole while dropping to the floor.

Learning moves that would entice our audience without bruising our knees was a huge task. I soaked in everything Mary and Ashley told us like a sponge so that I'd always have a fall back plan. Once she felt like we were ready we started putting on shows where we each took turns dancing in our bras and panties in front of the Pastor (my uncle), the deacons and any of the other men *or* women who wanted a good show.

We would all meet in the basement of the church on the days there was nothing going on. Doors opened at 7, the show began at 8. They would line their chairs up theater style and toss money at us as we danced. Having lessons with just Ashley and being in front of a large group of people, that you all know, are two completely different feelings. I was comfortable with Ashley, but once I got in front of everybody I felt ashamed and filthy for having money thrown at me. I listened as they said everything Ashley said they would and more. It was harder to ignore than I thought it would be. These were the same individuals I watched pray over people that were preying on us. Telling us everything they wanted to do to us and how they could please our bodies in ways we could never imagine. I felt like my uncle had been duplicated in multiple forms and I was trapped in a room with them all. Ashley gave me a few shots of Tequila to calm my nerves, but I still felt the same way. When it was my turn again I went into a zone, tuning out the people around me. Desperate times called for desperate measures.

Every dime I made was another step towards securing my escape. I only had to do this a little while longer. Soon, the day would come where I would be away from them. In the meantime, I was learning everything I could so I would have as many skills as possible to rely on later.

Mary and Ashley would supply us with whatever we needed then dock our pay for the amount of the expense later. I kept a bottle of Vodka or Tequila hidden in my room. That Saturday we had another event at church. I started inhaling shots before I went to church so I would have the strength to endure whatever took place. I had a different feeling this time though. Instead of the normal sadness, I felt this anger. Actually, it was a borderline rage brewing on the inside of me, but I ignored it. When I walked downstairs my aunt and uncle were sitting in the living room. She called me in to her and told me to get her some water. I walked around the house, went to the kitchen, grabbed a cup and rinsed it off. When I walked back I said, "We got three kinds of water. What kind do you want?"

"Three kinds of water? Where we get three kinds of water from?"

"I want some cold water. Go get me some cold water" she demanded.

"We got sink, toilet and refrigerator. It's all cold so which kind you want?"

"BITCH don't play with me! The damn refrigerator…" she yelled!

"Hmm… Ok then".

I walked away like I was going towards the kitchen, but as soon as I was out of sight I be-lined to the bathroom filled her cup up with toilet water, took her towel wiped the outside of the cup down, walked back into the kitchen, spit in her cup, opened the refrigerator door then closed it again. I did all this so she would think that's where the water came from. I opened the freezer, dropped a few ice cubes in her cup, mixed it around and served her with a smile. As she began to drink she commented.

"MMMMMMM…. This is good and cold. You can get my water more often. What did you do to get it so cold?"

"Nothing… It runs cold. I just added some ice to it." Neither of them caught what I said. My uncle grabbed her cup.

"Baby let me get some". He started drinking.

I couldn't hold the laugh in anymore. I bent over holding my stomach laughing. She snatched her cup back.

"Stop! That's mine. You gone drink it all." I walked out the room still laughing went to the kitchen to make them one last treat before I left. Both of them loved lemonade so I made them urineade (lemonade mixed with urine). I went to the bathroom, peed in a small juice bottle I had, then took it to the kitchen and began mixing. The urine went in first. I drank a lot of water so it wasn't that difficult to hide the pee. The scent wasn't strong and it was light yellow. I hid what little scent it did have by adding a can of frozen lemonade, sugar, and a few freshly squeezed lemons. Mixed it all together smelled it to make sure it smelled right poured it over two glasses of ice… AHHHHHH Refreshing! Served them both with their own glass to taste then returned to my room because I couldn't contain the laughter. Moments later they called me back downstairs because it was time to head to church. When I reached the bottom of the stairs my uncle slapped me on my back

"NIECE that was the best glass of lemonade I ever had. That's ya job from now on"

"I'm glad you like it!" I said with a smile. "Ha! Sons of Bitches" I said under my breath.

As we headed for the church I listened to them talk about everything that would be going on tonight. I couldn't tell you what was going on in the service because I spent my time running around, putting on private shows in the classrooms, as usual. After church was over Reverend

Timothy Marks was trying to eavesdrop on a conversation I was having with another young lady. Instead of inquiring on what we were talking about, he snatched me up by my arm and started yelling at me. That move triggered the rage already brewing on the inside of me and before I knew it I had completely snapped. It was like I had stepped outside myself and reacted. I yanked away from him, cussing and screaming at the top of my lungs.

"DON'T PUT YOUR MUTHAFUCKING HANDS ON ME! I DON'T KNOW WHO THE FUCK YOU THOUGHT I WAS BUT IF YOU WANT MY ATTENTION OPEN UP YA MUTHAFUCKING MOUTH AND SAY SOMETHING! BUT DON'T YOU EVER PUT YA GOT DAMN HANDS ON ME!"

Someone went to get my aunt, uncle, and some of the other ministers. Things were going from bad to worse quicker than they could respond. By the time they ran to the sanctuary I was already gone mentally…

He was pissed that I embarrassed him so instead of backing down he yelled

"BITCH YOU WANNA COME AT ME LIKE YOU GROWN I'M GO BEAT CHA ASS LIKE YOU GROWN!" He reared his fist back and swung. I ducked out of the way and punched him with everything I had in me. I watched as his head snapped back, he stumbled a little. Before he could react, I hit him again and kept the blows coming. With all the strength in me I kept swinging, each time landing head shots! Out the corner of my eye I saw my uncle moving towards me so, I started to move too. I bumped into the pew and saw it move. That was just the out I needed. I picked it up and swung it at them, hitting Rev. Marks so hard it knocked him into my uncle. They both went down. I pretended not to see my uncle and kept swinging the pew screaming "DON'T FUCKING TOUCH ME!!! DON'T NOBODY EVER FUCKING TOUCH ME AGAIN!!!" over and over. My rage made me feel like I had superpowers and I didn't know how to control them. My aunt stepped in between everybody and said

"Baby calm down. It's ok."

"MOVE!!!" I roared!

"Baby calm down. It's ok I won't let anyone touch you. I promise. Just calm down. Look at me!"

I was boiling and I didn't want to calm down. Deacon Ryan and a few others held me down as I continued to try to get to Reverend Marks while I screamed "BITCH I'M GONE FUCKING KILL YOU!" When they saw I wasn't calming down they finally just picked me up and started carrying me outside, still screaming. I guess they were thinking the fresh air would do me some good. I managed to wiggle free enough to jump down out of Deacon Ryan's arms. I hit the ground running full speed, charging up the aisle at Reverend Marks who was standing with my uncle. I dove at him, tackled him to the floor and started swinging. The fight began again. I held onto his hair as tight as I could and kept slamming his head into the steps at the altar. My body was in the air as they pried my fingers from his hair which eventually came with me. The bald spot I left in his head put a smile on my face as they carried me away screaming once again.

"Damn! This little muthafucker is strong! Shit I'm tired" Deacon Ryan said.

I guess I just had too much pinned up inside me. My aunt, Mary, and Ashley did everything they could think of to try to get me to calm down by repeating

"Calm down its ok. Everything is ok."

"No it's not ok! I'm sick of muthafuckas doing any and everything they fucking want to me and I'm supposed to just be ok with it! Fuck all you sorry sons of bitches!"

I snapped as I took off walking down the street. Still cussing and screaming, I was talking to myself but loud enough for them to hear me. I wanted them to think I had just completely lost my mind even though I knew exactly what I was saying at that point. Ashley chased behind me and walked me back to the church. My uncle walked outside and told me to let Rev. Marks drop me off at home so we could talk about what happened. I looked at him as if he was speaking a foreign language. If my face could have twisted up any tighter it would've. I glared at him.

"You know what… I see you two got me fucked up with somebody else. Fuck you and Rev. Marks. Both of ya'll can kiss the crack of my ass after a real good shit!"

Mary chimed in "That's your family. Don't disrespect your family like that."

I said "I got as much respect for my family as they got for me. They already taught me family don't mean shit. To them, I'm just another bitch in their house." I looked towards my aunt and uncle "Right? I gotta get to work. I got bills to pay. Right?"

They stared at me with their mouths hanging open. I walked away and started down the street. Ashley caught up with me walking again and slipped the cash in my hand from her and Mary for working that morning. It was chilly and dark out. Rev. Marks' wife pulled up on the side of me trying to talk to me.

"Look sweetie, I won't touch you and I won't talk to you if you don't want me to. But, I can't let you walk out here at night by yourself and you live across town. Let me drop you off at home".

Since she wasn't letting up I got in the car with her. She started talking to me. I kept yelling at her

"There is a way to do things. If you want to talk to me, open up your mouth and say something but don't put your hands on me. I'm sick of everybody wanting to put they hands on me! Don't fucking touch me!"

"I won't touch you and you're right." The rest of the ride home was silent.

As she drove, I was on my phone texting Stacy everything. Little did they know my last day of school was two days ago. That would be the last time any of them would ever see me again. We had two services that day so I knew they wouldn't be coming to the house till late that night or early the next morning. I called Stacy, who had been waiting a few blocks away. As soon as Reverend Marks' wife was out of sight Stacy ran in the house with me. We started packing as quickly as we could. I didn't have much so it didn't take long. We piled the most important stuff in her car first since her car was small. The remaining items that wouldn't fit I threw in the garbage. I didn't know if my aunt or uncle would ever come looking for me but I was going to make sure they never found me. I never looked back on my life there. It was time to start a new chapter.

Chapter 10

As we rode back to Lexington I gave Stacy the complete rundown of everything that had been going on. She didn't respond to any of it. She just stared at me in disbelief. I stopped talking and began staring out the window until we pulled up at the house. It was late and cold so we unloaded the car as fast as we could.

Soon after getting settled into our new house I noticed our neighbor was selling a 2010 sky blue, Buick Skylark. I knocked on the door and inquired about purchasing it. I was super proud because this was my first grown up move since leaving my aunt and uncle's house. It was a few more months before my eighteenth birthday and this car would be a birthday gift to myself. They couldn't transfer the title to a minor so I waited patiently until my birthday to get the papers transferred over to my name. In the meantime, I started attending Rock Vine Community College.

When I started going to college I didn't know much about it or about the process. I just knew it was the next step after high school, so I rolled with it. I picked a general major because I wasn't exactly sure what I wanted to be in life. Everything I knew to become wasn't really a profession I wanted to have. I hated the commute by bus every day, especially in the winter. But, at least I had something to look forward to. The winter weather made my decision to by a car even more special. I was pumped! I was going to school in style! I had been in school just under a year but I was already almost finished with my Associates degree in

Communications. I had doubled up on my classes from the start and attended school straight through the summer. I thought I was doing it big!

Since we moved to Lexington we found a church called Saint Mark Presbyterian and started going there almost immediately. After being in church for almost a year doing nothing, I finally decided to start participating in things. Since I loved to sing I joined the young adult choir. Pastor J.C. Clinton was the leader of the young adult department as well as Stacy's boyfriend. He might as well have moved in he was at our house so much. It didn't bother me though because the three of us would sit and hold conversations about all sorts of things in life. I had also started working for one of the ladies at the church. Minister Tiffany Barrels introduced me to everyone as her goddaughter. She had her own cleaning company called Make It Right Maids. Most of her clients were church members and with each client she raved about how awesome and amazing they were. Typically, we carpooled to a job sight. One day we went to clean Minister Matthew Holding's house. He was a single dad of four and had a huge two-story house.

As many times as I had seen him around the church I never paid him much attention. Really, I remember seeing him in passing a few times but never truly noticed him until that day. When we first arrived at the house he opened the door, welcomed us in, and asked if we would like anything to drink. I declined the offer. We both started cleaning downstairs as he sat in another room watching television. Usually, when Tiffany and I worked together we always stayed on the same level, if the home had multiple levels to it. It had been that way since day one. We'd knock out one floor then move on to the next. This particular day was no different. We started out on the same floor cleaning then Tiffany switched gears mid-stream. All of a sudden, she says

"I'm going upstairs to clean. I want you to stay down here and work."

"But we normally go one floor at a time. What's up?"

"Nothing's up! I want to try something different and see how it works".

Although I felt uncomfortable about it and wanted to press the issue I didn't. I decided to just go with the flow convincing myself that she must've been in a hurry.

As soon as she went upstairs Matthew came in the room and started talking to me.

"Hey beautiful?" I didn't respond "Hello Karen"

"Hello"

"I heard you weren't from here"

"Nope"

"How are you adjusting to our beautiful city?"

"Fine"

"You know I'm not from here either"

"Ok" Not really wanting to engage in a conversation, I kept cleaning as he continued to talk. After so long I noticed that he was moving closer and closer to where I was. Still, I continued to clean and didn't think much of it. Suddenly, he rushed me and tackled me to the ground. Fear instantly shot through me! My stomach felt like it was being stretched in multiple directions at the same time and I wanted to vomit. Did this BITCH just set me up?

I wondered. What am I gone do? How do I get out of this? The questions kept pouring in with no answers. I can't believe this is happening again. Why me? I fucking hate me and whatever it is they see in me!

I was wearing a long black, cotton skirt with the

matching t-shirt. As a result of him tackling me and me trying to get away, my skirt raised to my thigh in the front. It was up even further in the back. I could feel the carpet on my butt. This whole situation took me by surprise. This 6'3, 300 lb man had me pinned to the ground! As he straddled me he pinned my hands above my head and started dry humping me until he locked my arms together. He slides back a little. He was heavy on my legs and it hurt. I started to panic. Yelled for help. I heard nothing. "Tiffany… Tiffany… Help ME… Tiffany please I know you hear me! Help Me Please" wiggled, trying to break free. "Tiffany… Please Help ME… I need your help!" I yelled again but still nothing.

With his free hand he pulled my skirt up further and began touching me between my legs. He was laughing as I tried to get free. "Man dude… man get the fuck off me!" I continue to struggle. He exposes himself, reaches back and pulls at my panties. "HHHEEEELLLLLPPP Me!" I'm furious but I'm scared. I'm holding my breath waiting on him to rape me. I exhale and yell again "Tiffany… Please HELP ME! I'm begging you man please Help Me!"

A tear fell. I knew she could hear me. The house was too quiet for her not to hear me! The only sound being made was from the tv playing lowly in the next room. Just before he went inside we heard footsteps and he stopped. I lay there on the floor, balled up and scared. I called for her again. Still she didn't come. I continued screaming for Tiffany to come help me. He looked back at the stairs to see if she was coming to my rescue. When he realized she wasn't, he continued. I wasn't giving up. I continued to scream for her. Finally, she came down the stairs. He jumped off of me, sprang to his feet and straightened himself up before she reached the bottom. He stood against the wall, laughing. As she entered the room I was getting up off the floor.

"Took you long enough! So you didn't hear me screaming

for you?"

"Yea, but I thought you were just playing"

"Did you hear me laughing or screaming for you?"

He interjected "We were. I don't know why she was screaming for you like she was crazy. I was just tickling her" he reported while laughing hysterically.

"Why would I play with a grown man? Have I ever just randomly started calling your name and screaming for you to help me and was just playing? WE weren't playing at all."

"I don't know why she's so upset. I'd never do anything to hurt her. I was only kidding around."

"I don't either. I know you're a sweetheart" she batted at him.

Now I'm raging! "Sweetheart… Ok… What the fuck I'm gone lie for? You the same muthafucka that said trust me. Everything gone be alright from here on out. The same one that was praying with me over my issues and you the same bitch that left me hanging! You know what… don't even worry about it. It's good… I got you."

I couldn't believe she completely ignored the fear in my face and sided with him. I was scared and didn't know what to expect next but my fear was hidden behind my rage. By the way this conversation was going, it was confirmation for me that they had it planned out all along. She finished cleaning his house and then mysteriously her car wouldn't start. He offered to fix her car for her after he dropped us off. Not only did this sorry excuse for a minister and man just attack me, but now I'm going to have to get in his vehicle. During the car ride I sat quietly watching the trees pass by my face. I could feel her looking at me but she didn't speak. By the time we reached the house I went from being scared to being beyond pissed at her. As we got out of the car in front of her house she waved goodbye to him. I waited for him to pull off before I left in case he tried to follow me. Once he pulled off she finally spoke.

"I'm sorry you're upset"

"Yup" I responded.

I took off walking down the street. My walk transitioned into a full-blown run. I was trying to get away from her house and back to mine as quickly as possible. With tears pouring from my eyes, I couldn't breathe. I was so hurt. I loved her. I looked up to her. She knew so much about my life. Once again, I loved and my love was betrayed. I stopped running and bent over on the curb trying to catch my breath. A lady walking by stopped

"Are you ok sweetheart?" she asked as she gently placed her hand on my shoulder. When she touched me, I jumped into the street and just started crying even harder.

"Are you ok?" She asked again.

"No!"

"Do you need help?"

"No… Do you know what my life is like? I wish I was dead! Can't nobody help me! Ain't nobody helped me before now. It ain't nothing nobody can do."

I took off running again. She stood there and watched me till I could no longer be seen. Every passing car I thought could be him, so I hid. Once it passed I'd run again. I did that till I got home. I ran in the house, slammed my front door and headed straight for the shower. The artificial apology didn't matter. The damage had already been done. I didn't realize that Stacy and J.C. were sitting in the living room on the couch watching everything. When I got out the shower, Stacy came into my room as I was getting dressed. She sat on my bed quietly watching me for a moment before she asked.

"What's wrong?"

"Nothing!" I said in an irritated tone, with tears flowing down my face.

"Well, if nothing is wrong then why are you so pissed off? What happened?"

"Nothing… I can't believe her. I'm beyond done." More tears flowed. Finally, I told her everything that happened. She shook her head.

"I don't even know what to say behind that one." Stacy walked out of my room and closed the door. We never talked about it again.

As much as I never wanted to see Matthew and Tiffany again, as long as we were at the same church it was inevitable. We were supposed to have a revival that weekend and I really wanted to go. As much as I dreaded seeing them I still went. I walked right past Tiffany as if I never knew who she was. When she spoke to me I pretended not to hear her. She made it a point to cross paths with me and speak each time. So I moved somewhere else in the church when I saw her coming or either I would continue to ignore her all together. Pastor Marla Stevenson, one of the associate Pastors, noticed that I was ignoring Tiffany whenever she said anything. She knew how close we were so she inquired as to why. The first few times I went around answering the question but finally her persistence wore me down. I told the whole story. Her response left me speechless. As soon as I finished talking she questioned me.

"Well, what were you wearing?"

"A long black skirt and black top"

"Well, you know it was your fault, right?"

"Uh…No!"

"Yea, it was your fault it happened."

"How was it my fault?"

"You were asking for it. You are always walking around here dressed so provocatively."

"How is a long, loose fitting skirt and t-shirt provocative?"

"Tiffany told me some of the stuff you been through and I completely understand why things like that is happening to you. You were dressed provocatively and enticed him. You got a heavy sexual spirit that keep calling them type of people to you. It's called a sex enticing spirit. You got to deal with you to get rid of it. It's not their fault it's yours. I'm gone pray it get out of you but as long as you keep dressing the way you do and enticing these men, things like that gone keep happening. You better hear what I'm saying to you. That's a spirit in you that you really need to deal with and since you haven't yet you must like it. But I'm gone be praying for you to get that spirit out of you."

"How do I get rid of this spirit?" I needed to know.

"Child, that's between you and God. But like I said, I'm gone be praying cause a spirit like that gone get you in a world of trouble."

With a blank stare on my face I stood there speechless. Feeling heartbroken and confused I held back my tears. I could feel my heart beating faster and faster as my mind raced. Church was ending and I knew I had to get Stacy's car back to her so she could go to work. So, I decided to quickly make my way to my car, only to be greeted by Matthew. Flooded with emotions, I got in my car, put it in reverse and began backing up. As I entered into the street Matthew stood in the way of me being able to move forward.

"MOVE!" I demanded.

"I need to talk to you…"

"FUCK YOU! You ain't got shit to say to me so get the fuck out from in front of my car!" By now more and more people are pouring outside.

"I'm not gon' tell you again… Get yo bitch ass out from in front of my car or I'm gone run you over!"

"No! You gon' listen to me."

He must've thought I was playing because he continued to stand there. As I stared at him everything I felt that night rushed me at once. I reversed my car a little further so that I could gain some good speed then stepped on the gas. I could hear people screaming at me "KAREN NNNNNOOOOO!" I continued to accelerate. He still didn't take me seriously. He thought I was going to stop. I ran his ass over and kept going! The last time I saw him was as he rolled under the wheels of my car.

God,

I'm crushed… Pastor Stevenson confirmed everything my aunt said. Everybody wanting me sexually is all my fault. This whole time I've been walking around with a spirit in me that's asking for them to screw me regardless of what I say. This spirit is calling to them. Enticing them… but I feel horrible every time somebody acts on this spirit in me. It hurts like hell and I need it to leave me. My skirt went to my ankles. It wasn't skin tight. It was loose fitted. I didn't ask for anything. I told him to get off me… to stop. I fought back. I yelled for help. How was I enticing? Help me make sense of all of this. Help me find someone to tell me how to get rid of this spirit I'm walking around with. How do I get it out of me? All the showers I took afterwards, I still feel filthy. I can't just wash it away. Please God take it out of me. I don't like it and I don't want it. Please God I'm begging you…. Help me get rid of this and let me know when it's gone. On the flip side of things, I hope I killed him but please don't let me go to jail! When I saw his face, all I could think about was that day and now this spirit Pastor Stevenson said I have. What did I do to get it and how do I get rid of this spirit?

I prayed this prayer constantly in hopes that it would be answered quickly. I also prayed every day that no one would find me appealing. I prayed that every person that looked at me only saw my ugliness because that's all I felt inside. I had just become a modern-day Jezebel and didn't even know it. I thought if I changed my appearance it wouldn't happen again. I stopped wearing women's clothes altogether. If it wasn't baggy or loose-fitting clothes from the men's section I didn't wear it. All this happened the week before my 18th birthday. I told myself I wasn't going to let them ruin my pre-birthday celebrations, no matter what.

Chapter 11

However, I am so glad I didn't have my car yet. When I ran Matthew over it was with Stacy's car. I hoped that I didn't get her in any trouble because my friends and I planned to celebrate big. We had the whole weekend planned out. The first thing I was going to do was buy my car that morning. I couldn't wait. The morning of my birthday I woke up early excited. I ran to my neighbor's house to get the paperwork for the car transferred over to my name. When I got there, they were already waiting on me. They gave me a birthday card with $50 inside and the key to my car! The day was getting better and better by the moment. I picked up some of my friends that I met at our new church to grab breakfast then head to school. They were on cloud nine about my car because they didn't have one yet and we all hated catching the bus. I got to school just in time to receive my two refund checks. One was for $4,535.68 and the other for $875.22. I also had a half day because I tested out of two of my classes. So, I flossed my new ride around town. Then, we all headed to the bank to switch my account from a student account to a regular one since I was grown now. I deposited one check, cashed the other and headed to the mall!

Around 4 o'clock I received a text from J.C. asking me to give him a call as soon as I got a chance. When I called him back, he said he just wanted to wish me a happy birthday and wanted to know if I could stop by his house to pick up my gifts. I told him it would be later on that evening because Stacy and I were going to hang out for my birthday. He asked me to come before I went to pick her up from work. He wanted to talk to me about something important and he needed to say it privately. I agreed to meet up with him at about 5:30 since Stacy didn't get off till 7.

When I walked in the door I was blown away! There was a bouquet of red balloons, a dozen red roses, a beautiful candlelit dinner on the table and a card with $500 inside. I started to cry. I said "thank you! But this was way too much. You didn't have to do all of this." No man had ever done anything like that before. I didn't know what to think.

"I did all this for you because you're special. I've known how special you were ever since the first day I met you. I've always been attracted to you but I knew it was inappropriate. You were a minor so I just made sure you knew I was a friend you could always rely on."

I was flattered and confused all at the same time. He invited me over to the table. We said grace and began to eat the beautiful meal he prepared as we talked. There was shrimp, grilled chicken, pasta, dinner rolls and a wonderful chef salad.

"How can you be attracted to me when you're with Stacy?"

"Don't get me wrong. I really love her but I just can't help how I feel about you. Now that you're eighteen you should partake in your first glass of wine."

I readily agreed! After dinner I shared another glass of wine with him. I felt a little woozy so I thanked him for everything and told him it was time for me to go. Before I moved any further, I paused and asked him what he needed to talk to me about privately. He said I'd find out soon enough. I didn't give it a second thought.

As I was gathering my gifts, he came up behind me. This was beyond wrong, I loved him but not like that. He was more like a father figure.

"I'm not into older men and this is wrong" I said as I pushed him away.

He grabbed my arms and with an unexpected force he threw me on the couch. I was shocked! I never would've seen this coming. Until this moment, I thought it was an innocent birthday dinner, but as soon as I hit that couch all this became a familiar scene being played out again.

"I invested a lot of time in you. Now, I'm going to teach you what true love from a man feels like. You're a woman now and you need to learn."

Why the hell did everybody feel like I needed to learn this? This was a lesson I had no desire to ever be taught again. I tried to get up from the couch. He threw me back down then grabbed my legs and snatched me towards him. Before I could try to get up again he was on his knees. I struggled then stopped.

It was in the midst of me struggling to get up that I realized I was fighting another losing battle. I decided that before I let another person take from me I'd just give it away. I stopped fighting and surrendered to him. I tried to rationalize it and justify it to myself. I mean, everybody else was having sex anyway. I have to start sometime on my own, right? My battle turned within. Though I was convincing myself to surrender because fighting would only make it worse, I couldn't just completely let go.

I tensed up and scooted back on the couch. When I did that, he put his mouth on my panties and began gnawing. My panties were immediately soaked. I pushed back again and he pulled me towards him as he took off my panties and continued. Before I knew it my body felt extremely warm, my heart beat increased rapidly, and I screamed from the pleasure of the warm juices that gushed from inside me. J.C. raised his head.

"That's what it feels like to cum like a woman and you tasted just as sweet as I always knew you would."

He took my hand and placed it on his penis and said, "now I'm go teach you what it feels like to be fucked by a real man."

He flipped me over on the couch with my knees deep into the cushions. He rose up behind me and slid his fully erect penis inside me. I damn near lost my mind! It hurt but it felt great all at the same time. I moaned and groaned like I had heard others do with me previously. As I did he began to move faster and harder inside me. He pumped and pumped.

"I love you… you have the best pussy I ever had!"

He let out a loud grunt and we exploded together. Afterwards I couldn't bring myself to look him directly in the eyes. He told me I needed to go wash. I hung my head and asked him if I could use the restroom. As I washed myself, I thought about what just happened. I felt like the worst person on earth. I felt like I deserved everything that happened to me in life because of what I had just done. Once I finished cleansing myself, I grabbed my things and retreated to the door. I heard him call my name but I didn't stop. At that moment, there was nothing I wanted to possibly talk about.

As I was running to my car my phone rang. It was Carla calling to wish me a Happy Birthday. She was my best friend from back home. We had been keeping in touch the entire time I'd been gone from Carmel, Indiana. Due to everything happening in my life we lost touch for a while. When we reconnected it was as if we were never apart at all. The moment I heard her voice I broke down in tears and let her in on what had just happened, along with all the madness in my life. It was a little weird because she was the first friend I had ever actually told the extent of things to. As close as Stacy and I were, she didn't even know everything. She could barely handle the parts that she did know so if she knew everything she'd be emotionally unstable. Therefore,

I limited what I said to her in order to spare her.

Carla and I started talking about me moving back home. At first, I didn't want to do it but due to the most recent series of events, I decided I would go ahead and leave. Not quite sure when I'd leave or what I'd do when I got there I had to figure it out. There was nothing for me to go back to there. Nevertheless, the same thing I had here was what I'd have there…. NOTHING. So why not give it a shot? Maybe a fresh start was exactly what I needed in order to find my place in life. A life I no longer wished to be in. I needed a place where I could fit in and belong which didn't exist in Kentucky.

As I hung up the phone with Carla, I headed home and cussed myself out for what I allowed to happen with J.C. I picked up Stacy but told her I didn't really feel like shopping and just wanted to go home and lay down. However, she insisted we go to the mall, so I took her shopping. During our trip my mind was definitely preoccupied. This was certainly not how I imagined entering into my eighteenth birthday. I knew two things for sure. I was ashamed of myself and things would never be the same again. By the time we got home I felt like the weight of the world sat heavy on my shoulders and it became hard to breath and move. I sat in my room and cried till I had no more tears left to cry.

Finally, I got up to get some more tissue to blow my nose but instead picked up the razor blade off the sink. Running my finger across the blade I watched the small slits appear in my skin one right after another. Then I moved further up my arm. I thought to myself a paper cut is the worse type of cut you can have because its small and almost invisible. I figured if I could get use to this type of pain then as life continued to hurt me it wouldn't hurt as bad. So, I sat there cutting my arms and thighs watching the blood drip down waiting to become immune to the pain I felt. Before I could numb myself Stacy walked in

"KAREN!!! OH MY GOD!!! What the hell is wrong with you? Are you trying to kill yourself?" she snatched the razor blade from my hand.

"NO but the thought crossed my mind. I can still feel the pain and I need it to go away"

"And slicing ya ass open is gon' make that happen"

"You don't get it"

"You damn right I don't get it! But me and my baby need you here. I want you to see her when she's born. I don't want to have to tell her stories about you and the first time she meets you is in a grave."

We stared at each other in silence for a moment. She grabbed some washcloths

ran them under the hot water, placed them on my arms and legs, and pressed them down to slow the bleeding.

"I wish I was dead friend… I wish I was dead…"

"I know hun… I know… but one day life will get better. Just keep praying" We never spoke of that moment again.

When I went back to church the following Sunday, I completely ignored all of them. I told myself I was over it. I didn't want to have anything to do with anybody there ever again. In my mind, Matthew and Tiffany were in cahoots on setting me up to be attacked and I still couldn't wrap my head around what happened with J.C. I just tried not to think about it. If I never saw them again in my life it would be fine by me.

In that same service, Stacy informed Pastor Moore that she was pregnant. He was the head of the church and her mentor. Stacy was so elated but he wasn't. He was pissed at her and told her he didn't know how she could be so damn stupid! We were both confused as to why he was pissed off until Pastor Moore got in the pulpit. He announced in front of the entire church that Stacy was pregnant by J.C., who was a married man with kids. With that, he turned to J.C.'s wife and apologized to her on their behalf. She had finally shown up to a church service and this is what she walked in to. Stacy and I looked at each other in shock and disbelief. Then Pastor Moore called Stacy a home wrecker and condemned her for being pregnant by a married man. He put them both out the church! Until that moment, neither of us knew J.C. was married. He practically lived at our house so how could we have known? The entire time they were together he had Stacy believing he was divorced and had his wife thinking he was away on business. His wife and children attended a different church. I was embarrassed for her. Her feelings were so hurt. I felt even lower because that meant I had betrayed two people instead of just one. I was just in his house and saw no traces of a woman or children!

In the midst of my mind racing with thoughts and trying to determine if the signs were there, Stacy stood up as tears streamed down her face. She addressed J.C. in front of the congregation.

"I didn't know you were married because you told me you were divorced. Since you were at our house every day, all day I believed you. I had no reason not to. Mrs. Carson, I apologize for the disrespect and embarrassment being served to you right now, but I honestly had no idea about any of this." She turned her focus to Pastor Moore

"You knew the whole time I was dating J.C. It was never a secret. As my mentor and Pastor, why the hell didn't you just tell me instead of letting things get this far. Why would you let it come out this way? Why would you then chastise me in front of the entire congregation? Like any of this is a shock to you. Why would you do this to me?" We got our stuff and walked out. There was nothing I could do to help her. Hell, there was nothing I could do to help myself. I couldn't take any more.

The ride home was quiet. As soon as we walked in the house, Stacy laid down on the couch. I lifted her up, sat down, laid her across my lap and rubbed her head as she cried. Minutes felt like hours passing by as she sobbed. I wanted to talk to her but mostly we sat in silence because I couldn't think of anything to say. Eventually, I told her I was sorry she had to go through this but I couldn't do this anymore. I couldn't be in this state any longer. This was the straw that broke the camel's back for me. I was leaving tonight but would keep in touch. Part of me wanted to stay and help her heal her broken heart but I didn't see how the broken and damaged could be a stable support system to another wounded person. I had nothing to offer her. I went upstairs to pack, loaded up everything that could fit in my car and started driving.

The road seemed to be never ending and the trip got quite boring after a while. Too much time listening to the thoughts inside my head. They played louder than the music blaring from the radio. By night fall I could feel the broken pieces of my soul stabbing at my heart. I drove alone at night in complete darkness, wishing I had someone to talk to and no plan for where I was headed. I knew one thing for certain and two things for sure. One... Life had to get better at some point because I desperately needed for it to and Two... There had to be more to God than what I knew. More than what I had experienced on my quest so far to find him. So, I decided to talk to him while I drove.

Dear God,

My mama always told me you were real. I'm trying to know you, but all your people keep hurting me while I'm trying to find you. So, what kind of God are you really?

Since I can't see you in the physical I'm supposed to see you in other people, right? Aren't your people supposed to be a representation of you? Well If they are then I don't think I really like you. But I'm gon' do what I got to do because I need to see my mama again and the only way I'm go see her is through you, all I've become is their garbage dump so, which one of them will connect me with you? I don't know if you're really real but if you have my mama with you like everybody said you did, then I'm gon' keep trying to find you so I can see her again. I miss her like crazy. I was a mama's girl. She was my best friend. Why did you take her from me? Didn't you know I still needed her? I've never felt a hurt like this before. I feel like I'm dying from the inside out but something in me won't let me quit. I thought about killing myself today but the last few times I tried I failed. Since I'm sick of failing I just quit trying. Why am I here? Can you kill me too so I can get away from your people? I don't understand any of this. Why do I have to lose so much of me trying to know you? People talk about all these miracles you do but all I see is sex, drugs, money, and pain. I'm tired of crying. My twat hurts from all its unwelcomed visitors. Why am I going through this? Is this what it takes to know you? If so, I don't know how much more of this I can take. These tears are coming so fast I guess I better stop talking to you so I can focus on this road.

Amen

Chapter 12

After driving all night, I finally made it back to my hometown. I called Carla as soon as I was entering the city and asked her where she wanted me to meet her. I couldn't wait to see her! It had been years since we laid eyes on each other. We met up at a JoJo's Fajita Palace on the eastside. When we saw each other it was like life stood still. In that moment, we ran to each other screaming with tears streaming from our faces that felt like small waterfalls. She asked me where I was staying. I said, "my car". I didn't have anywhere to go. Well, she wasn't having that.

She was living with her grandma at the time so she would sneak me in at night and sneak me out in the morning before her Grandma woke up. I knew this set up couldn't last long so we started applying for colleges just so I could have a place to stay. I had to withdraw from Rock Vine Community College when I left. Carla also wanted to feel like she had her freedom. I didn't care who replied as long as someone with a dorm room took me in. I felt like since I was back home I'd do something all the way new. I was swallowing my past down hard and locking it away. I would try this life thing again.

I got accepted into Crossroads Central College. It was an all-girls, Christian college on the outskirts of the city. The school was decent, but I was just excited to have a bed to lay in and a door to lock. Carla was in the room across the hall. Living in the dorms was a whole new world for me. All of my credits from my previous school transferred over so I only had a year to be there. Unless... I went directly into another major to extend out my stay, which is exactly what

I planned to do.

I vowed that I was never going to another church again and I didn't for a long time. But, there was a church service that Carla wanted to go to and she was scared to go alone. She begged me to go with her. Even though I didn't want to go I did it for her. This is where I met Evangelist Lisa Marie Bradley, who made herself known to me as soon as I hit the door. She talked to me as if she had known me my whole life. Her great sense of humor was like a breath of fresh air! Within days of us meeting she let me in on her secret.

She was gay. It surprised her that I wasn't bothered by it. In actuality, I just didn't care. I loved who she was as a person and the rest wasn't none of my business. That was between her and the God she served. We had a lot of open conversations where we talked about our pasts, our dreams, and our goals. My only goal was to be able to lay in a bed each night for as long as possible. I hadn't planned out much past that. Lisa really liked me and had no problem letting me know it. She was very direct and since it seemed like men just wanted to take from me, I decided to try women. I started with Lisa…

As it turned out, she was a member at the church around the corner from where I stayed. I loved hanging out with her and every so often her best friend Valerie would hang out with us also. Valerie was a Minister at another church in the neighborhood. Lisa was so gentle towards me that she actually made me feel human again. She would tell me how much she loved me and how beautiful I was. Being used to feeling like the ugly duckling, it felt good for someone to come along who made you feel beautiful. It was something different. The feeling was amazing yet it was hard hearing all the compliments. I couldn't get used to it. How she felt about me didn't match how I felt about me. What she saw in me, I couldn't see. I'd stand in the mirror for hours trying to find what she was looking at. All I saw was ugliness staring back at me.

I remember the first time she kissed me. I felt scared. Everything had always been so hard and forceful so though I welcomed the gentle touches I wasn't used to them. I didn't even know if I was doing it right. I felt weird but just followed my instincts. It was the most awkward thing I had ever done in my life because I didn't consider myself to be a sexual person. She started kissing me while taking my clothes off. I could hear my heart beating... it was going so fast!

As she kissed down my body I kept jumping. It was too gentle... too soft... I kept bracing myself for something more to happen. I was afraid but I didn't want her to know. I learned early that no matter what, you didn't show fear and you didn't cry. Petrified to say "no" I let her keep going. I closed my eyes and kept giving myself pep talks in my head as she went lower. "Breathe... It's ok... This isn't like before... There's no roughness... You can handle this..." I said to myself. My nerves were getting the best of me and I couldn't hide it. Her gentleness was too foreign to me. My hands trembled... my body jumped at every caress... I tried to make it stop but it wasn't working.

"Relax. It's ok... I got you" she said as she continued going lower.

"Ok, I will..." I whispered trying to control the shakiness in my voice.

I relaxed as much as I could or at least I thought I did. Each time she moved against me I'd tell myself "try to enjoy it, relax, you're fine". A tear fell. I quickly wiped it away.

"You not saying anything..." she said.

"Oh, I'm sorry" I replied.

She got up and handed me my clothes. I put them on and sat there with my head down. She placed her hand under my chin and lifted my head up. She pulled me towards her and told me something I didn't expect.

"You know what?"

"What?"

"You really not gay. You're pretending."

"I could be…"

"Yea… you could, but you're not. You just following love wherever it takes you. One day you won't have to try so hard, but I'll love you whether you're gay or not and… I'll keep your secret."

We laughed and she held me and we watched movies the rest of night. We still talked ever so often but we didn't hang out as much after that. After a few weeks of us not talking, I received a phone call from Valerie. She was pissed!

"How the fuck you gone play my best friend!"

"I didn't play anybody. What are you talking about?" While she was talking, I call Lisa on the other phone.

"Hey baby what's up?" She answered.

"What the hell is wrong with Valerie? Why is she on my phone screaming at me that I played you?"

"Girl don't pay her no attention. She tryna figure out why we not together no more because I said it just didn't work out. So, she jumped to her own conclusions and now she showing out. She's really upset because I tell her everything, but I won't tell her what happened between the two of us."

"Ok. Thanks! Talk to you later hun."

"Bye baby…" I hung up and came back to the line. Valerie never even noticed I wasn't on the phone. As she's talking I interrupt…

"Valerie I'm sorry but I don't have time for this. Whatever happened between me and Lisa is our business and it has nothing to do with you. So, you have a good night. I'm getting off the phone now." I hung up. She called back and I answered.

"Hello?"

"Bitch! I knew when ya'll started dating yo ass wasn't no damn good. God told me!" Click!

I hung up the phone again. She hung up and called back continuously for an hour and a half. She left voicemails until it couldn't hold any more messages. I played them and began deleting them. As fast as I could hit delete, she was leaving another message. Two hours later, I was beyond annoyed so, I answered again.

"Look! I been trying my best to be nice but Valerie you really need to stop calling my damn phone!"

"No BITCH! It's Minister to you…"

"So, you want to be recognized by a title you don't operate in? If I did something wrong aren't you supposed to be a person who would pray for me? Someone to help me turn my life around instead of adding to the foolishness?"

"You just jealous because I'm better than you and Lisa was better than you too. She should've never given yo sorry ass the time of day."

"Why are you upset and she's not? Do you want her or something? Girl, get off my phone with your stupidity!"

I hung up again. She called back but I didn't answer. She continued to call. After another hour went by I picked up again.

"HUH… WHAT THE FUCK DO YOU WANT!!!" I yelled.

"You got one more time to hang up in my face before I come beat yo muthafucking ass! God gone send you straight to hell cause he don't like you no way!"

"Yea, well I guess I'm gone meet you there. Cause you goin ta hell with gasoline draws on, sitting on a rocket to make sure you get there quicker. You ain't shit but a fake ass minister and you want somebody to respect yo title. Who you ministering to doing the same shit everybody else is doing? And if you think you can whoop my ass come on with it. I'm at 4808 N. Centerville Road. How fast can you get here or do you need me to come to you?"

"BITCH! The bible says touch not my anointing and do my prophet no muthafucking harm! Yo punk ass gone try to shit on his prophet?"

"No… I'm stating facts. I'm saying his prophet ain't shit! When I'm getting drunk you drunk before me. The people I fuck, you want too. When I'm getting high and pass it to the left I'm handing it to yo ass. When Tee 'nem went on the stealing spree, you was taking shit right along with him and running. You ain't no better than nobody else!"

"Yes I am cause I'm anointed! And the bible says all my sins are forgiven. So, it don't matter what the fuck I do because Bitch, God already forgave me!"

"So… he can forgive you but not me?"

"Naw Hoe! Because you still got an unclean spirit. See… me and God talk daily and he knew when he created you he fucked up cause you wasn't gone never amount to shit! He told me when me and him was talking."

I stopped arguing with her and got real calm. "Don't chu know I will fucking kill you… I will slice yo ass up and set you the fuck on fire… Oh He didn't tell you that since He tell you so much… Bitch let God tell you what happened with me and yo friend and get the fuck off my phone. I respect people, not titles. If you ever call my phone again I'm going to find you and kill you. So before you think about dialing my number back, ask God about me. This time I'm sure He'll tell you just how serious I am right now. Have a good night."

I hung up the phone, finished watching my movie and went to sleep. I guess her holy spirit told her not to ring my phone again because she never called back.

Chapter 13

The next time I saw her was at a church event. When she saw me walk in the door, she walked out and never came back to the service. I wish I had left when she did. We had already been sitting in church for three hours when the pastor told the ushers to block the doors and not let anyone out the sanctuary. He said no one was leaving until the whole church was speaking in tongues. I thought it was a joke at first until I saw the ushers actually get up, block the doors and usher everyone that was trying to leave back to their seats. Surprised that a fight didn't break out in that moment, I waited to see what was to come. He did this half preaching, half praying combo where he kept going back and forth between the two, all while screaming out JEEEESSSSSUUUSSSSSS!

Then he asked, "how many people in the room knew how to speak in tongues?" Not very many people raised their hands.

"Those of you who can start speaking them right now! Those of you who can't start imitating the ones who can until you get it. The spirit on them gone transfer to you then you go be able to do it too. Ain't nobody leaving this room until every last person in here is speaking in tongues. Block the doors so they can't get out!" The ushers moved in front of the doors so people couldn't leave. Another hour went by and people still weren't getting it but were ready to go. So, they started making up things to say that sounded like tongues.

"Aye God I-thought-I-shot-at-robo-cop"

"He-shot-john-he-shot-john-oooooo-he-shot-john"

"I'm-seeking-my-honda, I'm-seeking-my-honda, I'm-seeking-my-honda"

"EBT EEE Aye God BBB Oh TTTT ummmm"

"tie-my-bow-tie, tie-my-bow-tie, tie-my-bow-tie"

"Holiday-bow, Holiday-bow, Holiday-bow"

"Holiday-bow-tie"

Now for those of us who were listening carefully, you could tell that people were just running random words and statements together really fast while they jumped up and down, pretending to shout. Thinking that everyone was actually in the spirit, the Pastor got excited and started running around the church. It was the funniest thing I had ever seen! On his third lap around he started laying hands on the people that were standing around not saying anything. He pushed their heads back until they fell. A lot of them just laid on the floor laughing. When he started heading towards me I just dropped down and laid on the pew like I laid myself out in the spirit! I **DID NOT** want him to touch me! Service started at 5 in the afternoon and it was now 2 in the morning. This service was no longer funny and I was ready to go! I waited until the usher went to go help someone and I ran out the door. The people that had fallen on the floor saw what I was doing jumped up grabbed their stuff and ran out behind me. We looked at each other, laughed and said goodnight.

When I got back to school from the church service that morning, Carla and some of her friends were standing in the hallway. As I stood there waiting on Carla to get what she needed from her friend and talking to someone else, I hear Carla's comment.

"Damn she got a fat ass!" I was confused. I looked at Carla, looked down the hall and saw the girl, then looked back at Carla.

"Who?" I asked.

Not thinking about it, she responded. "Her!"

Another girl was watching me. She said, "Based off the look on her face, I take it she didn't know you were gay".

"Oh shit! I forgot…"

I walked off. I wasn't pissed at the fact that Carla liked women. I was pissed at the fact that we had been friends this long and she hid it from me. Everyone around us knew except me! We ran into each other in the bathroom a little while later. I didn't say anything to her. As I was leaving she spoke.

"So you hate me now?"

"No, I don't. I still love you. I'm just pissed at you because you didn't tell me. Everybody around us knew but me."

"I'm sorry. I didn't say anything because I didn't want to lose you as my best friend."

"Girl, I don't care if you fucking females, males, cats, or dogs, but I want to know about it. Hell, I ain't no angel! I got my own story to tell so why would I stop being your friend because of yours."

"Cats and dogs though…"

"Hell! I'm just saying people or animals I just want to know. You know all my business."

"But animals though…"

We laughed and walked out. She was my road dog. It didn't matter what happened between us. We were still gon' be friends. So, after finding out about her secret, she became who I did a lot of my experimenting with until I was comfortable being with anybody, no matter the sex. It was in her that I learned to master controlling my emotions and how not to show that I was completely freaked out when someone touched me. She taught me how to hype myself up mentally to get into what I was doing. If I couldn't get into it she showed me how to fake it. It didn't matter who she dated, she loved me and I knew I'd always be more important than any of them. Nothing or no one was gone change that.

Because of the way our relationship was set up, we could typically ask the other one to do anything we wanted. That was whether we wanted to or not. Her request of me was to go back to church. She felt like this church she was at changed her life and it would change mine too. She was fired up and since I had never seen her so hype, I decided to attend to see what the fuss was all about.

Carla had joined Promise Land United Methodist Church. This church always seemed to have something going on and she was always inviting me to an event. I saw how active she had become and how drastically she was changing since she had been going there. I started getting a little curious as to whether or not she had actually found something real. We had been alike for so long and both vowed we were done with church. I noticed that though she only hung out with certain individuals they always talked about God and actively read their bibles. They were really sweet and encouraging. I thought maybe, just maybe this was the turning point. Maybe this God guy was hearing me after all and I was finally going to learn about him for real.

At this church was where I met Robin. From the first moment we met we hit it off great. Robin, Carla, and I became inseparable. She and I had so much in common. Though our stories were different there were a lot of similarities. This is what made me feel like she could relate to me in ways and on levels others who hadn't been where we were could. It made loving her and trusting her easy. She was 10 years older than us, with her own family and life to live, but she took the time to invest in us. Especially me. She became someone I looked up to and admired. I watched her in the face of day to day challenges and she didn't really seem to let them bother her a whole lot. She used to always say she would handle as much as she could and the rest she'd give to God for Him to handle.

We used to have spiritual debates because I was at a point in my life where, when it came to God, I didn't believe in Him at all. I had been going to church all this time and nothing came of it. Prayed to God to get me away from the people that where hurting me only to end up around people that ended up hurting me even more. My philosophy was… "Jesus was just like the street pharmacist, just another nigga I keep hearing about with a temporary fix, but never there when you need Him the most". She'd say that He was so much more than that. He was loving and kind, a healer, a provider, a safe haven. I didn't understand that because I was never safe from anything.

She didn't mind the debates at all. Whatever I wanted to know she'd answer me. Robin was there for every problem, always offering up words of wisdom and encouragement, praying with us, counseling us. When all Hell broke loose in our lives, she was right by our side fighting for us, with us, and on our behalf. There was nothing we wouldn't do for her in return. She gave us the love and attention we always desired but never received. She knew everything about me and my past and loved me anyway. She would always say stuff to me like…

"You are such a beautiful person. I love you. You gone be my new baby!"

"Why?" I'd ask.

"Why what?"

"Why do you love me? You haven't even known me that long? I've always been unlovable to everyone else so, what makes you any different?"

"Because you're such a sweetheart. You're naïve, but you don't just give up on things right away. You keep going. You keep trying to figure things out no matter how hard things get and I love that about you."

Though I wasn't quite sure how to take that, I accepted it and I loved her too. When the financial coordinator at the school called me, Carla, and several other girls into her office to tell us that our money was running out, it felt like our worlds were falling apart all over again. We were going to have to start paying an additional $2,250 a semester in order to stay there. Everybody had someone to turn to for help except for me and two of the other girls, Melonie and Shelia. They reached out to their parents and church but couldn't get any assistance. Everybody told them to drop out and try again another time. I told Robin and she said she'd work on coming up with something. We needed a plan and quick. We only had till the end of the semester to figure things out and that was less than a month away.

Melonie suggested we go strip, but no one really knew how or what to do. I said, "I do". Everyone was shocked! I told them I learned how to do it at one of the churches I was at and explained to them what to do. I showed them almost everything I learned. We even went to the fitness center on campus to do weight training exercises so they could support themselves on the pole. We decided that if we were gone strip we weren't going to any of the strip clubs in our city because we knew all the people there.

We went out to the strip clubs in the surrounding cities. Ones we knew none of our people would drive to. We made a killing! We'd bring home anywhere from $500 to $1000 a night, but it still wasn't enough. We were only going down on the weekends because that's when the clubs were the busiest. It seemed like the more money I made the faster it went. I could never generate enough cash to get ahead. One night at the club, some guys got aggressive and kept trying to get us to go home with them. Things started to escalate and they would no longer let us dance. They kept grabbing and grinding on us so one of the managers put them out. After leaving the club, those same guys decided to follow us. It was a little over an hour drive to where we lived and part of it was a dark wooded area. We were terrified. They kept blowing their horn yelling at us to pull over. We knew better than to stop. We couldn't go home either because we didn't want them to know where we lived.

We were flying down the highway and they were right on our tail. We saw a police officer and started slowing down a little. The guys were so focused on us that they weren't paying attention and got pulled over. We knew they were going to jail since they had been drinking. We were free! Let's just say that our stripping career was short lived. The money wasn't worth the risk. Since that was our only back up plan we were stuck. We went back to the dorms and started packing our bags because we could no longer afford to attend school. Robin was trying to come up with ways for me to be able to stay but she couldn't come through fast enough. I still had to leave the campus. I went to stay with some friends. One of my old choir directors Tasha, and her two sisters, Felicia and Kim took me in. We all hung out like sisters. I'd taken care of them so many times before. Now that I needed somebody they opened their doors. It didn't last long though. The first time I didn't go with the flow of things it was an issue.

Life had begun getting overwhelming. I was struggling to contain my emotions. People would never understand what was really hidden behind my smile. The never ending pain my heart experienced. I went from low to lower. I consistently fluctuated between two emotions... sadness or anger. When I did get an emotional high it left within minutes. So, I started smoking weed and drinking constantly. It could be 7:30 in the morning and I was turning up a bottle. I poured liquor into water bottles, soda bottles, and restaurant and gas station cups. I even had a flask. It didn't matter much to me. My only concern was that it didn't spill. Hell, it was five o'clock somewhere so my turn up was always real! It was my way of escaping from the world. I became so dependent on being in an altered state of mind that I needed it to function. I needed it to cope, but I also noticed that I wasn't getting anywhere in life. I always had to be cautious because when I altered my state of mind, I made myself an easier target than normal. I was like the prime prey on an open market and since my defenses were down, it made it easier to overpower me. Alcohol wasn't my liquid courage. It was my strength so that I could keep enduring when I wanted so desperately to die, but couldn't.

I needed to reinvent myself. I wanted to make a change and become something greater than everyone's garbage dump. I made a vow that I was going to write the best chapter of my life. Better than all the other chapters before it because I was only as great as I challenged myself to be. My first start at changing self was to change what I was doing. I stopped smoking and drinking. It wasn't easy the withdrawals from it were horrific but I fought my way through it mentally and physically. After so long, I didn't crave it anymore and I didn't feel like I just had to have it. Since I had developed a closer relationship with Robin, I started going back to church again and trying to get a different outlook on God. My friends couldn't stand the person I was turning into. They preferred the old me. The one that was willing to turn up with them at any given moment. I just didn't feel like being that person anymore.

Now, I'd never been one to just sleep with any random guy the first time I met him. For those that did… more power to them, but it wasn't for me. Everybody knew that about me and although it was ok any other time, this time was different. It became an issue because we no longer had anything in common.

"You won't fuck anybody, you won't drink and you won't smoke. So, what… you think you better than the rest of us now?" Tasha asked.

"No, but you must. That was never my feelings. I was just trying to do something different in my own life".

"Hell you act like you holier than thou." Felicia commented. "Since you done got 'saved' you want to turn yo nose down on all us and act like you better. When in actuality, you ain't nothing more than a hoe trying to find Jesus. So how about you find yo judgmental ass and self-righteous God another place to stay cause we don't need you… YOU needed us. Now you act like you forgot who you was and the places you came from. You ain't above gutter trash. You just gutter trash disguised as a Christian and as fake as fake can be" she proceeded to say.

I fought back the tears and swallowed hard, choking down my hurt feelings. How quick the tables turned when they no longer needed you. These were supposed to be my home girls. My squad… my ride or die niggas and they just flipped the script on me like I didn't even matter. Because I'm trying to turn my jacked-up life around? The fact that I just didn't feel like participating in their activities ain't enough. For whatever reason, they refuse to accept that. My feelings were yet again an irrelevant factor. They threw in my face that they took me in when I didn't have anywhere to go. The fact that I had been there for everything they needed was also an irrelevant factor. In that moment, none of that even mattered. My life didn't rest solely on their shoulders. However, I needed to buy myself a little time.

"I'm sorry ya'll feel that way. So when you want me gone by?"

"You can have till the end of the week."

"Yup"

I acted as if none of it fazed me at all. I still cooked, cleaned, and listened to them talk about me like a dog behind my back as I pretended not to be listening. I heard the lies they told of things I did. They claimed that these were the true reasons why they turned on me but it wasn't. They started spreading lies about me to anyone that would listen. They did all that not knowing I would not only find out about it, but could prove they were lying. Still, I didn't say anything just for the sake of trying to keep the peace.

I stopped paying the bills and didn't say anything. If it was due when they handed it to me, it was gone still be due when I left. It would be disconnected if it was in my name. I didn't buy any more groceries and pretended not to notice that my stuff was mysteriously coming up missing. Two days before I was supposed to get out, I came in and dinner was already made. Everyone was being so nice. Tasha was in the kitchen fixing plates for everyone. I figured that since she cooked, it meant I wasn't invited to the meal. But, to my surprise, she called me to come eat. I walked into the kitchen and saw everyone eating from their plates.

"There's your food… bon appetite!" She said as she pointed to the dog dish on the counter.

"Are you fucking serious? Is this shit for real?" I asked.

"I figured I would feed you like the dog ass bitch you are…"

"How quick do we forget who held you down and had your back all the times you needed me. And this is what you do…? It's cool. I got you."

She laughed as I walked away. It was amazing to discover what people that say they love you really think of you when you can no longer supply their needs. I never thought this would be my reality, but it was. The very ones that said they loved me and had my back were the very ones talking about me like a dog. They lied on me… crushed me… I was speechless. They thought they were all I had because I couldn't keep staying on campus. With or without them I was going to be ok, regardless. I walked out and went into the room that housed my stuff and started packing. As I packed my bags tears fell out of frustration. Kim came in trying to talk to me. I didn't want to hear it.

"That was wrong and you deserve better… they shouldn't treat you like that as much as you held them down when they needed it"

"You ain't got shit to say to me and you was just out there laughing wit em! It's all good. I got all you muthafuckas!"

In my book…to hell with all of them. I felt worthless. All that because I didn't want to follow along? Because I wanted to do something different or just because I wasn't comfortable with doing what was being done? It just wasn't me and I had lost enough of myself for someone else's sake.

They didn't get that but nevertheless; none of it mattered. In that moment, I didn't care what an Indiana winter felt like or how cold it was. When Kim realized I wasn't trying to hear what she had to say she left me alone. I listened to them laugh and crack jokes at my expense as I packed. See, she thought I was going to fight her but I had something better planned. My anger should've never been underestimated. I was so pissed I was calm. I finished packing and waited till I was carrying out the last bag. I shut the lights out in the room, balled up some clothes threw them on the bed and in the garbage can, poured a bottle of nail polish remover on the mattress, lit a match, tossed it in the garbage then lit another one tossed on the bed, made sure I saw the flames going closed the door and left. I never looked back. I hoped the whole house burned down with all of them cackling bitches in it!

My car became my home. On the nights when the

temperatures dropped down close to zero, I would bundle up under everything I had in the car till I just couldn't bare the cold anymore. Then I would let the car run with the heat on full blast till I unthawed, then cut it back off again. On the days I had somewhere to be I would wash up and dress in the bathroom of restaurants or at work just before my shift started. There were many times I went days without eating. I realized I could last two weeks barely eating at all. Sometimes I got lucky. I'd go visit someone who was willing to feed me, but more often than not I simply suffered in silence, praying for better days to come. I didn't have anything to prove to anybody and I didn't need anyone. I came in this world alone and would go out the same way. The in between was just something I needed to get through.

Chapter 14

I had been living in my car for months before Carla and Robin found out. Robin told me to come stay with her. When we became roommates it was like nothing changed between us. She continued to tell me that she loved me and how beautiful I was. I loved her to pieces but I felt that way about her long before we ever started living together. It seemed like our bond grew even tighter once I moved in. We were each other's support system. Whatever she needed, I made a way for it to happen. The same way I was there for all my friends. I followed love wherever it took me because I needed it.

I didn't realize until it was too late that just because people say they love you, doesn't mean they're telling the truth. Sometimes they just say it to get what they want out of you. When I love, I love hard and I loved my roommate. We had been through a lot in our lives and she had been hurt so much. I could relate to that because I had been deeply hurt as well. When we decided to live together I was trying to escape the hell I was living every day. At the time, I didn't know I just went from one bad situation to another. Our pains spoke to each other and built the strength of our relationship. I was willing to do whatever was required of me as a friend. The closer we became the more she pulled me into her world. The more I got to know her, the more she drew me into her darkness with my love for her.

She eventually introduced me to Pastor Mitchell Bell, but when I met him it wasn't in the church. At the time I had no idea he was even a Pastor. I was just hanging out with my roommate and she told me she needed to stop and see a "friend". She needed to pick up something and it would only take a few minutes. I was ok with it because I was enjoying her company and didn't have anything else to do. We parked in this neighborhood and started walking.

"Where are we going?" I asked.
"Just come on, but if some shit jumps off I need you to make sure you got my back."
"Damn! You couldn't WB before we got here?"
"I'm warning a bitch right now! I'm just saying…"
"Oh, so that's why you parked around the corner? So your car can't get tore up?"

Though I wondered what we were walking into, I wasn't gone let her get hurt. I prepared myself for a fight and started to memorize my way back to the car in case we needed to make a run for it. I also scanned the area, looking for potential weapons in case I needed assistance. We walked up to the back of this building that almost looked abandoned and rung the bell on the side. The door opened and we walked up two flights of stairs into this apartment. A 5'8, muscular, bald, dark chocolate gentlemen greeted us

"Have a seat on the couch"

She introduced us. "Karen this is Mitchell. Mitch this is Karen."

We scanned each other up and down, said hello and shook hands. The gentleman escorted her to the back and I had a seat on the couch and began watching television. After a few minutes, Robin came and joined me on the couch.

"Would either of you like some water?" he asked.

"No, I'm good, but thank you."

"I bet you are" he replied.

I looked back at the television. When I look over again, my roommate is attempting to swallow his penis whole, with her mouth. I look back at the television again.

She takes his penis out of her mouth and asks…

"You want to try it?" Looking at her as if she'd lost her mind I reply "Naw I'm good. You got that… that's all you boo!"
"I don't mind" He says.
"I bet you don't, but I'm good. Ya'll gone and do what you do."

She continued what she was doing and he begins to moan. I tried to concentrate on the television as hard as I could. They laughed at how focused I was on trying to ignore them. She pushed me over on the couch.

"I know you feel me looking at you…"

"Ok and…?"

"We're gonna leave in a few minutes, but I really want you to try this."

"Naw, you got it. Gone and finish…"

"I said… try it!"

This time she replied in a stern voice. I tried to pretend as if I wasn't nervous. "No".

"It ain't like you a virgin hell somebody done already fucked you?"

"Just because somebody fucked me doesn't mean that now I'm a bobble head…"

"Do you even know how ta suck a dick?"

I turned back towards the television and ignored her. She continued to suck again until he was satisfied. Once he was pleased, we left. She yelled all the way back to the car.

"I can't believe you got in there and choked up like a little bitch! He's gone be around a lot so you better get used to it!"

"You was talking about fighting, not pulling out dicks and popping them in yo mouth like it's the hottest thing since sliced bread!"

"You gone have to learn how to please your man cause what you won't do, the next bitch will!"

"Well I'll worry about that when I get a man that needs to be pleased..."

"I'm trying to help you..."

"Thanks, but I'm good on the sex stuff."

"Look, I know you had a rough past, but you gone have to get over it and loosen up. You're too uptight and you can't let what happened to you make you scared of sex. I'm trying to help you get over your fears. Neither of us will hurt you. Everything you do with us, look at it as a learning experience."

On Sunday I got up and went to church with her and Carla. I didn't tell Carla what happened the day before. I almost fell flat on my face when I walked in and saw Mitchell. "He's our Pastor" Carla confirmed. He looked at me, smiled and said hello. I looked back at Robin, shook my head and took a seat. It amazed me how fast they switched in and out of these different character roles. Carla also introduced me to his wife and children. I never would've imagined that the man I met yesterday and the pastor I met today were the same person! Is this really typical church behavior?

Once church let out, Robin and Mitchell pulled me into his office to explain. Mitchell reported

"I'm still married but me and my wife are separated and have been for the last 18 years".

"Wait... How you separated for 18 years but you have a 3 and a 14-year-old?"

"It's complicated" I didn't say another word I just walked out. When we left church, Robin took me by their house and continued to fill me in on the details.

"But aren't you still cheating if they are still married?"

"No… because they have no intentions of ever getting back together. She doesn't want him anymore. She only stays at the church so he can see his children."

"Then if that's the case why don't they go ahead and get a divorce?"

"He's tried she won't sign the papers!"

"But if you don't want somebody and have no intentions of ever getting back together with them why not let them go completely?" She stared at me in silence so I turned to stare out the window. I wasn't sure what to believe but I left the subject alone. I started to see a lot more of him around the house though.

Robin woke me up early the following morning "let's go to breakfast." She suggests

"I don't have money for breakfast"

"My treat"

"I'm black… so, free food just got my attention!"

"When we finish eating I need to stop by the church. I need to get some stuff from my office and Pastor Mitchell wants us to clean up the half-way house across the street. Six guys are coming to move in this afternoon. The person who was supposed to clean up canceled at the last minute."

Little did I know, that day was going to be more than I bargained for. I would get more than breakfast out of it. We went to IHOP and sat in the restaurant laughing and talking. It started out as the best morning ever. Then we got to the church, went into her office, gathered her things and took it out to the car. We went across the street to clean up the half-way house for the new arrivals. As we finished, Pastor Mitchell came across the street, complimented us on a job well done and told us not to worry about the trash. He would take it out because ladies weren't supposed to carry trash. Robin and Pastor Mitchell disappeared across the street. I finished sweeping the floor, gathered the trash, put it in a bag, and went over to the church. As I walked in I could hear them talking in the sanctuary. They were discussing different projects to start within the ministry, the choir, etc. I proceeded down the hall toward the voices and sat on a pew near where they were standing in the isle.

While I waited on them to finish their conversation, I started going through my phone to find a game to play. When I realized that the voices had stopped. I looked up and my roommate had the pastor's dick in her mouth in the center isle of the sanctuary! My jaws dropped. They had absolutely no limits and no boundaries!

"Ya'll goin' straight to Hell!!! Do not pass go... Do not collect $200.00 Just straight to hell"

"Quit acting like a scared little bitch" she says. As she fussed at me, she took her clothes off and climbed her naked, mocha body onto the pew. On her knees she faced the pew and bent over. While still talking to me, he got naked from the waist down, walked up to the pew behind her and slid in. This entire scene made me sick to my stomach. I got up and walked out the sanctuary. There was a fear that ran through me and I had no idea what I was supposed to do in that moment. I went to the front door of the church to leave but it was locked! I walked back into the sanctuary to go to the back door to see if it was open.

"Why don't you join us?" He asked.

"Now, I know folks do a lot, but ya'll are out of control!"

I ran to the back door but it was locked too and they had the keys. Damn! I was trapped in here with them.

SHIT!!! "God open the door…. We all about to burn together!" There was nowhere for me to go. I went and sat in one of the offices near the window. I was praying the church didn't burst into flames with me in it. I was used to being scared but this fear was different. This was a spiritual fear. I just knew God was about to set the church on fire just like He did in Sodom and Gomorrah and I was gone fry with them! Guilty by association… He kept yelling my name but I didn't move. Finally, he threatened me.

"You ain't got nowhere to go and you not leaving out of here until you come see what I want!"

"I already know what you want…"

"You sure about that? You don't know shit! Bring your ass here!" He laughs.

I got up and walked back into the sancutary. They were still having sex, so I started walking out again.

"STOP!" He yelled. "You want to get out of here? COME HERE!" I went back but I didn't go near them.

"Don't be scared… come here."

"No, thank you. I'm good."

"Don't you want to join in?"

"HEEEEEELLLLLLL NAW!!! I'm good. Hell we know a Bitch a sinner but damn you about to get a bitch caught up!" They both laughed but I didn't see the humor.

"Well, I want you to watch what's gone happen so you can learn how to do it later."

Ok God,

Why I gotta keep learning these lessons? Why everybody feel the need to teach me this same crap? Since these yo people can't you tell them I'm good on these lessons cause FOR REAL I AM!

"You know…its some things I can go the rest of my life without ever knowing. Although this was nowhere on the list, because I never thought it would happen, it just made number one."

Robin finally speaks and says "come here Kay (her nickname for me)… it's ok. Everything is going be alright. I'm going to show you what you need to do."

"Naw, I'm good."

"Again I say, quit acting like a scared little bitch".

"Did anybody forget that we're in the sanctuary at church or am I the only one that noticed? You don't disrespect God's house like that. What is wrong with you?"

"So, you more afraid of God than you are of me?" Pastor Mitchell asked. I didn't say anything. I just looked at them.

They laughed and said, "God knows we're sinners saved by grace so, it's alright. God loves us just the way we are."

"I think you taking his grace for granted. I might not know a whole lot about God or religion but as a sinner, there's a whole lot we can do. But, disrespecting God in His house… it ain't something I'm gone participate in. Some places are off limits. The church got to be off limits."

I went to her office and closed myself in until somebody took the key and unlocked the door so I could leave. I did everything I could to block out the sounds, but the harder I tried the louder they got. This was one of many lessons that was to come. No one could prepare me for the things I saw. The funny thing about it was that this moment was the easiest of the lessons...

As we left that day, Robin was so annoyed that I

didn't join in.

"I let you stay with me, anything you need from me whether it's a listening ear, to wipe your tears or to feed you I'm right there for ya ass and you can't even do the simplest shit I ask you to do for me! All I asked for was one little fucking favor but naw that was too much!".

"That wasn't little to me and it didn't feel right."

"Fuck that if you really loved me like you say you do, then you would participate the next time I ask you! If you don't then I know the real deal and you just using me like everybody else did. I don't know what the fuck you scared of we'll teach you everything".

So, I made up in my mind that I would. I felt like with everything she had helped me get through emotionally, the least I could do was prove to her that I loved her. That I wasn't just trying to get her to do stuff for me or like I was taking advantage of her. So many other people had already done that to her in the past. I didn't want to be another one.

Chapter 15

With what I learned from being with them sexually, I started to feel like I was a pro. Even though I was participating, the church was still off limits for me. We would be in the middle of a meeting and she would slide under his desk and start sucking his dick. People would be walking in and out of his office and he would be sitting there trying to keep a straight face. He was teaching us how to separate our feelings from what was taking place. Once I mastered how to mentally separate myself from what was going on, it made extra room on the inside of me to store more stuff. Most of the time, when the three of us had sex, I was having a conversation with myself. I would tell myself to play the role and pretend like I was enjoying it. All I had to do was lay still and just relax.

However, there came a point when the conversations and alcohol wasn't soothing enough to me. I began to have trouble getting out of the bed on most days. I went to sleep praying that this day would be my last. I would wake up the next morning sad that my eyes opened. I had to have a pep talk with myself for at least 30 minutes just to move. At the end of the day, it didn't matter how I felt or what I was going through, all I had to depend on was me. The bill collectors ain't care nothing about my emotional distress. So, I kept drinking and I kept pretending like everything was ok.

In the beginning, I stayed because my need to be loved was deeper and more potent than the sacrifice that needed to be made. Unfortunately, the sacrifice became too great for me to bear. That's when I wanted out but had nowhere to go. I was trapped with no one to turn to and not enough money saved anymore to do anything. Every dime I accumulated went to someone else. My money went to the relationship I was in, the people I loved, the bills that needed to be paid, the cars that needed to be fixed, the food that needed to be bought. I always ended up in a situation where it appeared as if everything was riding on my shoulders and I couldn't bear to see the people I loved in distress.

After a while, I noticed that beyond me, Robin was bringing Carla into it. I took Carla on a walk and came clean about everything. I told her what was going on between Robin, Mitchell and me and warned her to stay clear. I knew the consequences behind being disobedient once you were in and I didn't think Carla was as strong as I was. I didn't want her to end up trapped in my situation. However, she didn't listen. She idolized Robin and Robin knew just how to play on her insecurities to reel her in. Once she sunk her teeth into you there was no getting loose. It seemed like for the longest time she had this emotional hold on us that weighed us down. Even if we were mad at her, all she had to do was cry and say we didn't love her anymore. We would go running to her trying to prove to her that we did.

Robin was always looking for new ways to keep Mitchell's interest. One night, it was decided that all of us should entertain Mitchell together and record it. Carla and I were dead set against it but Robin spent days on this tangent. She went on and on about how we didn't love her for real, because if we did the little things she asked us to do wouldn't always be such a big issue. I felt so uneasy about it all. The day everything was to take place, I was so nervous and unsettled. I walked into my room, sat on my bed and pulled Carla down next to me.

"I'm not doing it" I said.

"Why not? You know mommy really want us to" Carla replied.

"I told you to stop fucking calling her yo damn mama! Daughters don't eat mama's pussies!"

"Well… in those moments I block that out and I don't think about it."

"That still ain't cha fucking mama."

Just then Robin walked in. "Hey babies! What are ya'll talking about?"

"I don't want to do it" I told her.

"…and if she don't do it I'm not doing it either."

"Well you know I would never make either of you do anything you don't want to but I'd really appreciate it if you help me out."

I felt so heavy in that moment. She hugged me and held me in her arms. I laid my head on her chest. Tears slowly made their way down my face.

"It's ok" she said as she rubbed my back.

"I really need you to come through for me tonight and not leave me hanging at the last minute, but I understand. Don't do nothing that won't allow you to look at yourself in the morning. But if you do it, it would mean that you love me soooooo much and I'd owe you big time! I don't want you to be nervous. It's gone be ok. I'ma be right there with you the whole time."

"That's not just it. Yea I'm nervous but I'm also sick of sex. I feel like that's all I'm good for. Plus, I don't wanna have sex with you! I'm not attracted to you like that. I don't look at you like that. Any other time we were having sex with Mitchell we barely touched each other. This time you're requiring me to play a different role" I explained.

"Well you can imagine me to be somebody different or I can take the lead role and you just follow my lead. But, I love you sooo much…and I really need you to participate and do this for me. I don't ask you for much so if I tell you I need you it's because I really do. And if you do this for me I promise I'll never ask you to do this again. I just need you for this one night."

Though my inner voice was screaming "HELL NAW…" "ok" rolled off my lips through an abundance of tears. I felt like I would be wrong if I left her hanging, but I was sick of being an actress and nothing in me wanted to play this role. But of course, when night fell I obediently stepped into character and played my part to ensure their movie was a success.

As the four of us were having sex, it was getting worse and worse for me to handle but I was still going through the motions. It got to the point where I couldn't stomach any more. I wasn't sexually attracted to any of them and for some reason, faking it just wasn't coming as easy as it used to. This didn't feel like just pure entertainment. This was something else. I felt like an imitation porn star in a wrestling match of titties, asses, pussies, and a dick. I stopped and stood by the side of the bed, next to the camera. As I was watching them interact with one another I saw Mitchell hand Robin some cash. Was she pimping us out? Had I become a hoe with Robin as my pimp and didn't know it? I felt my anger rearing its ugly little head again. I went to the bathroom, washed, dressed and sat in the living room. I waited on them to finish so we could go home. They called me to come back into the room but I didn't respond. Robin came out and tried to talk to me but I wasn't trying to hear it.

"Why you leave? Come back in the room. We not done yet".

"I am. I can't do this no more. Are you pimping us out and calling it love?"

"No" she laughed. "I would never do that to you."

"Then what was the money for?"

"He was giving me money to feed us with after this was all over".

I didn't believe her. "Yea ok... I don't have the stomach for this no more. I'm done with both of ya'll. Tonight, was it for me".

"Oh, you think so... OK..." she replied and walked back in the room to continue. I didn't know what was gon' happen but I was ready for anything.

After that, every chance she got she would try to talk me into participating, but I wouldn't. She was also screwing another guy named Chris at the time. Whenever he came into town she would try to get me to have sex with her, him and his friend as well. She would get mad when I didn't. Because of my disobedience, she made my life a living hell. She cussed me out daily and told me how much she hated me because Mitchell said he preferred me over her. He told her I was tighter, wetter, and felt better. She said the only way he would have sex with her was if I participated. I didn't understand why she was so offended because I didn't want to participate. She shouldn't have wanted to either. He was sleeping with almost every female in the church! I didn't care. My answer was still no. Things had gotten entirely too crazy and dangerous. We were stalking people, slashing tires, busting windows and tearing up the cars of his mistresses. I was disappointed at myself for going down that road in the first place. I wasn't stepping back into it again.

During that same time, I met a new friend at one of our church services. A young lady by the name of Tiana came and sang. Tiana was 5'4 and dark chocolate with long black her. Her voice was so powerful. I felt like I was in a trance as she ministered. Listening to her, I became so consumed with her notes. Her vocal range was amazing. I loved it! After the service was over, I went to compliment her on a job well done. She and I started talking, exchanged contact information and started hanging out a lot. Robin couldn't stand it because it kept me away from her and Mitchell.

Tiana was the complete opposite of Robin and everybody in that church. She sparked a curiosity in me that made me want to know more about her. Her Christian walk wasn't like the others I had seen. She prayed for others instead of praying for materialistic things. She searched for the good in others even if it was sometimes difficult to see. She believed God could bring her through anything no matter how difficult the situation. She prayed constantly about everything. She'd stop what she was doing to pray for or with someone else. She didn't require you to tell her your entire story in order to know what to pray for. She listened to you and offered real advice instead of judging you because of the life you were living.

When she offered advice, she offered it from two perspectives… a spiritual view and a natural view. I respected that the most. If she said or did something that was wrong she didn't use the scripture to justify her wrong doings. She simply acknowledged and explained her feelings and apologized for being wrong. She read her bible daily and would sit me down to read scriptures with her. We'd each give our interpretation of what we thought it meant. Then she would bring it current and show how it could be applied to our real-life moments. She didn't push her religion on you but she believed in helping people see the importance in having a relationship with God.

When I told her what my Christian walk had been like, she cried. I watched in disbelief. Then she prayed for me that God would pull me out of the arms of the corruption. I loved that I was able to speak freely, openly, and honestly about the place I was in, in my life. I was constantly asking her millions of questions about God, church, religion, how to find God and whatever else I could think of. She would try to get me to visit her church, but I wouldn't go. I didn't trust the church or the people in it! She respected that so she didn't force it, but that didn't stop her from asking me to attend every so often. I know it was in hopes that I would finally change my mind. When I would say "no" she'd just say, "Ok I'll keep praying about it then".

I felt confused in my spiritual walk. I knew I didn't want to be in the streets because running the streets was just as dangerous as going to church. Yet, I didn't feel like I belonged in the church either. I knew too much about the corruption in it to make myself comfortable. I didn't trust nobody and when Christians were nice to me, I found myself looking for the other shoe to drop. I needed to know why? What were they after? When I walked away from all the live porn, I also walked away from the church. This royally pissed Robin and Mitchell off, so anytime I was away from Tiana they tormented me.

One day, as I was leaving the house, Robin made it clear that I had no more choices. She was sitting on the couch filing her nails. She tripped me and leaped towards me as I was walking past her.

"Bitch! I can't stand you! He prefers you over me and you don't even want his ass! You ruined my relationship! And now you don't even have the decency to fall in line with things. I regret ever letting you in my world!"

I felt something digging into my back, carving away at my flesh. Sharp piercing pains raced through my body as my skin started to rip. I laid on the ground trying not move. The pains were hitting me hard. She bent down and whispered in my ear.

"The next time I ask you to do something just say yes…"

As I'm flooded with pain, hurt feelings and rage, a bitterness filled the back of my throat and consumed me. I shifted the weight of my body to the left, throwing her off my back. As she fell back I see the finger nail file in her hand. Blood slowly ran down towards the handle. Drops of blood were dripping from the tip. She wiped the finger nail file off on my shirt. As she attempted to stand I lunged at her, knocking her back down to the floor. Overcome by the sadness I was feeling, the betrayals mounting, the rage that was consuming me was now front and center. I wrapped my hands around her throat and squeezed. My thumbs met on the muscle moving in the front of her neck. I pressed down as hard as I could, trying to snap it!

"BITCH YOU BETRAYED ME! You were supposed to love me but you lied…" my grip tightened. I felt these little hands beating at my back. I tried telling myself to stop but my rage had full control.

"Stop Kay stop you're hurting her!" this little voice yells "Stop it Kay please stop it!" She pleaded as she tugged at my shirt.

"You two love each other. Don't you? Get off my mommy… let her go!"

I looked up into this little face full of tears. The sins of a mother should never affect the child so I let go. Despite my new feelings towards her mother, I never wanted this little girl to feel the pain behind losing her mom like I did. Especially not caused by me. I looked at that sweet face.

"We used to baby… we used to…"

I got up and went to the bathroom to see how much damage was done. I turned around in the mirror and there was a long slit that ran down the lower half of my back. Tears started falling. I took a series of deep breaths to stop them. I was literally choking as I struggled to suck them all in. I walked to my room, pretending not to be bothered by the pains that ripped through my body as I moved around. I changed clothes and left. I prayed again as I walked out the door.

God,

WTF I'm mad as hell... I'm like pissed smooth the fuck off right now!!!! Every friend... Everybody that say they love me for real betray me... Did you create me just to hurt? Just to be everybody's trash bin? I loved her for real! I trusted her. I looked up to her. I did stuff for her to where I couldn't even stand to look at myself no more just to prove to her I loved her. And for what! She shitted all over me! I guess trying to know you just comes with pain. I don't know what hurts more my body or my heart... I feel like my soul shattered. There's pain in every breath I breathe. When I look at myself in the mirror all I see is a million-piece puzzle. It's all these little pieces laying everywhere. I have no idea how in the hell I'm gon' put me back together again because my heart and soul is torn into all these little ass pieces! How is this Christian walk supposed to be? Do you have anybody that's real? Is this type of pain all that being a Christian consist of? If so why the hell would anybody want this? What kind of God are you that you don't protect your people? Are you just sitting back watching this go down? I don't want to live, let alone live like this. If you real and you can hear me... help me get free... Help me out of this. Help me get away from these people. I can't take it no more. I'm dying on the inside. I need a lifeline or I need to just go ahead and die. So, can you either help me or kill me because I'm good with either!

Chapter 16

As I was coming down the porch stairs I saw Carla walking up the street. I met her a few houses away, grabbed her arm and pulled her away with me. We headed towards the back of the house where my car was parked, only to discover my car had been completely destroyed. Someone had keyed it up, busted out all the windows, flattened all four tires, and spray painted BITCH all over it. No use in saving it. It was completely gone and I didn't have any insurance. I knew who was behind it but couldn't prove it. I felt sick to my stomach. I knew things were going to probably get a whole lot worse before they got any better. I felt my emotions fighting their way out again, I took a deep breath. I couldn't afford tears right now.

"Oh My GOD!!! What the hell is going on around here? Who did this?" Carla was screaming.

"Come on. Let's go. Ain't nothing we can do about it now."

"What's wrong? Where are we going?"

"Walking…. Just come on!"

"Wait… Hold on… I need to go upstairs first to use the bathroom."

"Huh ok but don't let her talk you into staying. I need you to come with me. I'll tell you everything while we walk."

"Ok"

I waited downstairs for her to come back. When she did we went for a walk and I filled her in on everything that had been going on. Walking would become our daily ritual so we could say things openly that we wouldn't ordinarily get to say in the house. When all of us were in the house together I would walk past Robin as if she didn't exist. Ignoring her when she called my name… moving away from her when she reached for me. Days went by… the house was silent. I could hear crying coming from her room but I didn't acknowledge it.

"I've never seen you and my mama so sad before."

"I'm alright baby and yo mama got her own demons she's battling with but she'll be ok when she gets over it."

A week into the silence, while Carla and I were on one of our usual walks, my phone rang. A tearfully, frantic little voice was on the other end.

"Come quick! Come help her! Something's wrong with mama!"

I could hear screams and sobs in the background. "Ok! I'm on my way!"

Flashbacks of my childhood weighed on me as we took off running back to the house. Racing up the stairs, breathing heavy we ran into the stale smelling bedroom where she was balled up on the bed screaming! Though I could see that she was hurting I only partially cared. I put my arm around her to comfort her as I shooed the baby out the room.

"We got her. She's gon' be ok sweetie. Go watch TV." I closed the bedroom door behind her as she left.

"What the fuck is wrong with you? Whatchu doin all this damn crying and carrying on for?

"Don't nobody love me no more…" She whispered in between sobs.

"Oh… That's what the fuck I ran all the way back here for?"

Carla hit my arm as she reassured Robin "I still love you…"

"She don't…" Robin pointed at me.

They both looked at me waiting for me to respond. Carla bucked her eyes and her neck at me trying to get me to say something. "Look, you hurt me in ways I never thought you could. I'm not going to get over it overnight and I'm not gone pretend like none of it happened because it did. But, at the end of the day it doesn't matter how any of us feel about you, you still got a child that needs you. She's looking at you, watching you, worrying about you. So you got to pull ya self together for her. Fuck everybody else."

"But - I – still – love - you… I – miss - you…"

"Yep… I saw ya love first hand and it brought us here. I ain't saying I'm over loving you but I'm hurting in a real dark place that I ain't coming out of no time soon. So you need to get yo shit together for that little girl in there. Hell, love come and go so suck that shit up and charge it to the game as another day. Wipe yo face, clean this damn room up, and keep it moving. You gets no sympathy here for some shit you caused." I walked out her room into the bathroom, grabbed a roll of tissue, walked back in and threw it at her head.

"Here wipe yo damn face and shut up all that damn crying like you dying. Ain't shit wrong with you but some hurt feelings. Get yo shit together!"

 Carla walked out the room. "Do you have to be so mean?"

"I'm not being mean. I'm being honest and besides, at the end of the day didn't nobody give a fuck about my feelings. So what the fuck should I care about other muthafuckas feelings for? I'm sure ain't nobody ate. Here… take her car and go get some pizzas so they can eat."

Carla ran to the store. I cleaned up the kitchen, gave lil mama a bath and started braiding her hair while we waited for the food to arrive. Shortly after, Carla finally came in the door, placed the food on the stove then walked in the room with Robin to check on her. I fixed everyone a plate. I put Robin's pizza on a plate and took it into her.

"Here… eat something."

"I'm not hungry…"

"Well you done laid your sad ass around here all week and ain't ate nothing. Put some fucking food in yo system. HERE EAT!!!" I shoved the plate at her. She smelled it.

"Did you poison it?" She asked as tears fell from her eyes.

"Not this time, but if you keep fucking with me you bet not eat the next plate I hand you." I laughed.

"You hate me don't you?"

"Not yet but I'm close…" I walked back out the house again to meet up with Tiana.

When I finally made it to Tiana's house I told her what was going on. Among the many things she said that night, she told me I needed to figure out how to get away from them. I knew she was right, but it had to be at the right moment. I felt so lost and helpless so I continued to turn up the bottle for refuge.

I remember being hung over, severely depressed, and bitter when a Jehovah's Witness knocked on my front door. Normally, I would leave them out there because the ones that came to my house always wanted to argue or talk to you forever. I usually didn't feel like hearing it, but this particular day I figured I'd try a new brand of religion. I decided to listen so I opened the door.

"What…"

"Do you have a moment to talk?" the lady asked.

"I ain't got nothing but time" I replied as I sat on the stairs with my elbows on my knees. My face rested in my hands as I stared at this cocoa brown, 5'2 lady with long black hair. She began to speak. I saw her lips moving but I really didn't hear a word she said. I was too busy trying to suppress the thoughts in my head and swallow my tears. Finally, I interrupted her speech.

"Have you ever been so hurt and so broken on the inside that you couldn't tell your up from down? Didn't nobody want you... not even death?"

"Yes, I have and that's how I became a Jehovah's Witness" she explained.

"Girl, Jehovah probably don't want me either because I'm too messed up. I went looking for God because that's who they told me had my mama and I wanted to see her again. I got raped, sexually assaulted, turned into a drug runner, became a stripper, got pimped out...I was a hoe and I didn't even know it until it was too late! I woke up every day more depressed than I was the day before just because I opened my eyes... and I'M ANGRY! So here's the million-dollar question... what can yo God do for me that the other people's God couldn't?"

"Well, are you safe now?"

"Yea, cause ain't nobody at home right now but, when they come back that's a different story. But, I know how to survive. I've been doing it this long..."

"Jesus honey... I am so sorry and I know this ain't what we're supposed to do, but can I pray for you?"

"At this point you can do whatever you want. Everybody else already has so I don't even care anymore."

"Father God, in the name of Jesus, I come to you as humble as I know how... standing with your daughter, who desperately needs you God. Protect her from the evil that surrounds her and mend the shattered pieces of her heart Lord. Send her some help Lord because she needs it like never before. Place your angels around her to defend her against the enemy. She needs somebody on her side to help her get free. Heal and help her God. In Jesus name I pray. Amen."

"What the hell you doing outside!" a voice yelled from inside the house. I jumped.

"Go… hurry!" I told the lady.

"Nothing… I was talking to the Jehovah Witness. She was praying."

"Stop doing that damn lying! They don't pray! Get yo ass up here!"

"Hell, they might not, but she is…Ok" I walked back in the house. I heard the lady take a deep breath and sigh as she watched me walk away.

"Go hurry…" I told her again.

"At least go stand on the other side of the street." I didn't want her to get caught up in whatever was about to jump off. She did as I said. I closed the door and walked back into hell…

Chapter 17

On Thanksgiving, I was home alone and depressed. Tiana called and told me to meet her at the church so we could talk. After arguing with her for almost three hours about how I didn't go to church anymore, I gave in to her persistence and went. As I entered the building my heart started racing. I was nervous and scared. I thought the church was gon' catch on fire because I walked in. Once I actually got inside it was like I had entered a whole new world and I didn't realize it. As I walked through the building, she was sitting in the kitchen on top of the deep freezer. She hugged me when I walked in and we started talking. The other women in the kitchen were cooking and fixing plates. She introduced me to everyone in the room. They were either her aunts, cousins, or friends. Not too long after I got there, a beautiful caramel slender frame lady walked in and hugged everyone there. She spoke to me and I waved hello. I don't know what it was but a fear ran through me when I saw her. I didn't say too much after she came in. Even when I tried not to look I could still feel her eyes piercing me. It was as if she was looking straight through me.

All of a sudden she grabbed a chair, flipped it around, squatted across the chair with her arms folded on the back of it and asked

"Why do you hurt so bad?" I just looked over at Tiana who said, "answer her… it's alright".

"Are you serious?"

"Yes I'm serious…"

"Do you really want to know?"

"Yes, I do."

Everybody in the room had a look of shock on their faces, as if I had just said something wrong. A lady whispered, "she's the Pastor and this is her church". Then Tiana told me the woman I was talking to was the assistant pastor, as she giggled. I said, "so you set me up?" I was annoyed. I headed for the door, but they blocked the doorway. I started freaking out. I held my breath and tried to walk out the door. The women moved again to block me from leaving. I took another breath but my breathing was increasing rapidly. I was starting to panic.

"Coming to church again was a bad Idea. I gotta get out of here."

"No… wait… don't... Ladies, move out the way. Don't block her from leaving."

She kept talking to me and though I could hear her, she sounded so far away. I was trying to slow my breathing down. She asked the question again.

"So why do you hurt so bad?"

Though my mind was telling me not to say anything, before I knew it, my lips spewed it out.

"Because every day I'm living in hell and that's all my life has ever been! I found my mama laying in the house dead when she was supposed to be with me forever. Church is where I learned to sin professionally. I was just trying to find God so I could see my mama again. I've been raped, beat and sexually assaulted. I'm barely surviving, enraged, devastated and dying inside. I got real monsters I see daily that haunt me with my eyes open, I…"

"Shhh….. Stop…." She interrupted. "I'm going to touch you."

She took my hand. As we began to walk out of the room, I looked back at the other ladies. They all looked sad. Some of them even had tears in their eyes. They could tell I was scared to go. I looked to Tiana for reassurance. She looked into my eyes and said "go… it's ok." I felt a little pull on my hand then began to walk again. She lead me to the other side of the church to her office. As she closed the door she could tell I was starting to panic again. She spoke softly.

"You're safe. I'm not going to hurt you. Tell me what's going on?"

Normally I wouldn't have said anything but I was at a point of not caring. If anybody could help me get out of the state I was in, I was gon' take it. We talked for three hours that day and met every Thursday at 10 a.m. after that.

It seemed like every day I went home I was walking into more and more drama. It wasn't safe. One day, as I was walking down the street, Mitchell pulled up on the side of me. I knew he had to be nearby watching the house because I had only made it a block and a half before he rolled up on me.

"Get in the car".

"No thank you…"

"Get your ass in the car!"

"NO!" He showed me the gun sitting on his lap

"Get yo ass in the got damn car now!!" My heart sank and I thought I was going to die. I listened and got in. He started driving.

As he drove he said "Now listen… you don't want to come back to the church? Fine, but you ain't going to nobody's else's church either. Especially not the one you been hanging out at. Stay yo ass away from that church!"

He pulled up at his house and told me to get out the car. He walked behind me as we moved toward his place.

God,

If you up there and you hear me… I know I said gone and kill me but please don't let me die like this. But if this is how you gone take me out can you make it quick and painless? I know it's been a while since we talked but please… hear me… I'm alone and scared.

He took me to his room, made me undress and lay down. He sat the gun down on the dresser and had sex with me until he was tired. The whole time he moved inside me all I could think about was how to get him so caught up in the moment that he wouldn't notice me reaching for the gun. None of the scenarios playing out in my head looked like they would work so I just laid there waiting for him to finish. When he finally did, he told me to get dressed and dropped me back off a few blocks from the house. He warned me not to say anything to Robin. I tried to act as if everything was normal, but it wasn't and I couldn't. I woke up later that night with him on me again. My night gown raised, panties ripped, and him telling me how I liked it. Days went by before I could even mentally tell myself it wasn't a dream.

God,

They told me if I continuously talk to you, you'd eventually hear me. I had sex yesterday. Even though I said no, it happened anyway. Stripped out of my clothes I laid there naked, cold, and empty. My heart felt like it had given up. I didn't put up much of a fight. I just allowed it to happen. I'm not even a fan of sex but it's so much easier to give it up than to have it taken from me again. I'm so tired of feeling someone go inside me. I feel myself slipping away more and more and I need something to grasp hold to. I refuse to further lose myself in this one... sometimes two individuals.

I didn't stop going to the other church though. They seemed like they really cared about me. They were doing more for me than I was doing for them and didn't require anything of me in return. Had I really found the for real for real Christians I was looking for? It felt good to be wanted but not needed.

In my next meeting, I told the pastor they were following me and about the things they were doing. After the first few weeks of us meeting, Mitchell started having me followed consistently by his girlfriends at the church. I would run down streets and through alleys, trying to escape the detail. It seemed like no matter where I went I wasn't safe, but no matter what happened, I kept being drawn back to that church. I was so impressed by our weekly meetings that I started going to the church on Sunday's for service and Wednesday nights for bible study. It was nothing like where I had come from and every service was more and more intriguing.

I wanted to give up on God and the church. I would even stop going for months at a time, but something in me just wouldn't let me quit. My spirit wouldn't die even when I felt dead on the inside. They were the closest thing I had to Jesus and I still wanted to know him better. Except... I was at a point where I was completely and utterly devastated. My eyes told on me constantly and there were very few people I was fooling. I tried to appear as if everything was ok and I wasn't being fazed by the things that were happening. My eyes were telling my truth though. I was shattered on the inside, hurting far beyond what anyone could imagine. I spent my days looking over my shoulder in fear and watching my back.

One night, I awoke from a deep sleep to someone grabbing me by my ankles. I was snatched from my bed. My head pounded and my neck ached from hitting the floor so hard. Startled and scared, I slid across the floor backwards towards the wall. It was Mitchell and Robin standing over me. After staring at me for a moment he finally spoke.

"I was having you followed and I know about the new church yo ass been visiting. I know what days you there and what times you go. You gone keep being hard headed and you gone write a check yo ass can't cash. Now, I done already told you to STAY THE FUCK AWAY from there and you still going up there to that damn church!"

I didn't say anything so he continued.

"Now, I'm trying to help you. Warning comes before destruction so your little ass might want to take heed. Stay the fuck away from that church!"

I still didn't respond so Robin took a belt and started hitting me with the buckle. She hit me while asking me if I heard what he was saying. In between blocking my face from being hit, I tried to reach out for the belt in hopes of grabbing it away from her. I screamed out "YES… YES! I hear him!" Tears rolled down my face.

"Then next time open yo fucking mouth and respond" she said.

Ok God,

I can't keep doing this I need some help for real. I know they don't want me at the new church but I can't stay at this church with them. They said if I keep talking to you, you gone eventually show up. Well, I need you to come running up in here asap! If you can't get in here I need you to send me a whole gang of folks to come knock they ass out! I hate them and I hate church. The church is supposed to be a safe place and it's not. I live in hell daily. I got real life monsters living in my house that I have to face. I'm tortured mentally and physically and I leave the house come to church and sit in hell trying to find Jesus. Church should be my escape but it's just as bad. I know I'm supposed to look past the mess to hear the messenger but the messenger is as messy as the congregation. I'm stalked, threatened, physically assaulted, and raped. I'm the port-o-potty for the saints to relieve themselves in while teaching me the spiritual relevance. They do whatever they want while using scripture to justify everything they're doing and when I don't follow suit I'm next Sunday's message. Yet I'm at the church every time the doors open because I have to be. Because if I'm not, I might miss my opportunity, to meet Jesus and if I missed my opportunity I may never get the chance to see my mama and I NEED TO SEE MY MAMA AGAIN. Why do you hate me so much that this is what my life has become?

I did as I was told for a while and started going back to the church with everyone else. The church had been having a revival all week and Robin played every Christian role there was to be played. She was the greeter, the usher, the cook, the administrative assistant and the list goes on. She'd been on her feet all day and looking in her face I could tell she was exhausted, but I didn't care. I figured the more tired she was the less likely she was to add more hell to my life. As everyone was clearing out of the church, she asked me to help her finish cleaning the kitchen so she could go lay down. I ignored her the first couple times but I noticed that she had completely slowed down. That meant we would be there forever. Since she was my ride home I gave in and began helping her. I was beyond ready to go. She smiled and told me it wouldn't take too long. There was only a little more to do.

I rolled up my sleeves and began moving as fast as I could. I just wanted to get done. I cleaned off the tables, took out the trash, then returned to wash the dishes. I was looking at the pile thinking… *I can't wait till I'm finished cause I will never wash another dish again.* As I washed, I thought about my life, everything I had gone through and the place I was in. I was thinking about how deep I was in all this mess and trying to figure out how I was going to get out of it. I was so deep in thought I didn't even hear him coming. As I moved to the corner, reaching to grab the next pile of dishes, my trance was suddenly interrupted mid reach by the feeling of warm breath on my neck. My first instinct was to run but I was trapped.

Before I could turn around or move I was pinned against the sink, between two counters. A hand was around the front of my neck squeezing tightly while my breast were being groped. The back of my neck was being licked rapidly all while my ass was being humped. It was so disgusting and humiliating. I tried to speak but dizziness started to set in due to the lack of oxygen. As I was being choked, I could feel my pants coming down in the back. I remember thinking… maybe the moisture of my tears would loosen the grip from around my neck. I kept jerking my body from side to side trying to break free, but I could barely breathe.

My mind was racing a thousand miles per minute… who was this? Why was this happening to me in church? He slightly loosened his grip on my neck. I was trying hard to catch my breath when I felt the worse pain I ever felt in my life! I thought my vagina was being ripped apart! I felt burning and extreme pain all at the same time. I let out the loudest scream I could muster up, but then he wrapped both of his hands around my neck. He squeezed tighter and tighter, I became light headed and knew for sure I was about to die.

It felt like I would pass out at any minute so I waited for the darkness to consume me. He was thrusting vigorously inside me. The pain was unbearable. With every gut wrenching stab of his penis, I felt like my soul was being ripped away. I felt my flesh tearing. Although this wasn't how I wanted to go I prayed this would be the moment that death finally welcomed me. I didn't want to have to face the reality of this moment once this ended. Just when I thought I couldn't take it anymore I started getting light headed. It felt like there was no more air left in my body. Thankful that I was escaping this nightmare, I told myself "just stop fighting and die". At that very moment… he stopped. Holding on to the counter coughing and gasping for air I mustered up enough energy to turn around. When I saw his face, my body just sank to the floor. I was in a daze. I was lost and felt hopeless. It was Pastor Mitchell! As I was able to regain control of my breathing I mumbled between sobs.

"Why? Why me?"

He replied "Because everybody in the bible went through something and you're not any different. Besides, God knows our heart. As long as you do right by me you're doing right by the will of God."

Devastated doesn't even begin to describe what I felt. The rumors came right behind it. The very ones that said they loved me passed them on to people that didn't know me at all. Rumors started by the people in leadership that I hung out with. People who were loved by so many that whatever they said was law. Passed on to people that didn't know the hell I was going through in real life, but everybody had something to say about me. About the change in my behaviors, my mannerisms, my appearance, the way I reacted to people, how I looked. I was called everything except my name and compared to every animal in the jungle.

They didn't know what my life consisted of, yet everybody had something to say about who they thought I was. People didn't understand how their words or actions affected me. I didn't even understand it for a while. I was so accustomed to listening to the stories surrounding the pews but I never thought I would've become one of the tales. It didn't even matter if it was true or not. When you're on the other side listening to those stories, you don't think about how the things being said affect the other person. That is…until it's you.

I began to relate to why Kelly killed herself. It made perfect sense. When a person is already going through hell and feeling weak and vulnerable, you could be the very thing that sends them over the edge. Your words… Your actions can crush the little they were left holding on to and cause them to take their own life. A lot of the time, people feel like they have the right to say whatever they want because they have freedom of speech. They think that people should have a thicker skin, but what do you do with a pain that's unbearable, unbreathable, unmovable, unstoppable? A pain that keeps stabbing away pieces of you but you can't stop the blows. It just keeps cutting at you until there's nothing left but a hollow shell. Having a thick skin is irrelevant. A person can only take so much. Everybody, no matter how thick their skin is, has a breaking point.

I smiled and laughed at some of the jokes made about others, thinking the jokes at their expense were harmless. Suddenly, these words were like sharpened swords that sliced through me, leaving rows of wounds with stinging flesh. Yet, no one cared. They kept it coming.

"Hey everybody! What's a garden tool that everybody uses?" James asked.

"A hoe!" Michael laughed.

"Hoe… oh you mean Karen?" Brenda taunted.

"I'm not a hoe…" I protested.

"What does bungee jumping and Karen have in common? They both cost a hundred bucks and if the rubber breaks, you're screwed!" Brenda continued.

"Yea… you a hoe. I heard you tryna make yo way to first lady cause you want a better life, but hoes transition not transform!"

"Bitch FUCK YOU, You full of shit!"

"No, I'm not. In the last meeting, Mrs. Mitchell charged up Robin about sleeping with her husband. Robin told her she had her confused with you cause she wasn't messing with Pastor Mitchell. Pastor Mitchell confirmed it and said you were trying to hit on him but he turned you down. He said you look at him as a fast come up but it was nothing for her to be alarmed about. He would never allow anything to happen."

"These lying ass muthafuckas…." I blurted out, but was cut off before I could finish my thought.

"Don't you know it's a proper protocol you got to go through to get that position? You got to go down on all the other leaders first." Sister Shelia chimed in.

"What the fuck? That's some bullshit and they both lying. I don't want his ass and I never did!"

I walked away and took a seat. They sat behind me still making comments and telling Hoe jokes at my expense.

"Twinkle twinkle little whore, cheaper than the dollar store…" They laughed and sang.

"I know you hear me. You can't ignore me forever! What does the wind and Karen have in common? They blow everybody!"

"I mean… I'm not saying you're a hoe Karen. But, if your vagina was food it would be a free sample at the mall in the food court."

"Ok here's one… You ready?"

I heard Mary but before she could get it out I cut her off. "Who got more money… the drug dealer or Brenda? Brenda… because she can wash her crack and reuse it! How come when Brenda die they gone have to bury her in a Y shaped casket? Cause every time you lay her on her back she opens her legs." A roar of laughter erupted!

"Brenda… I'm a hoe but you suck more dicks than little kids suck popsicles. As a matter of fact, you were just downstairs going down on Deacon Roberts in the choir room on the low cause you wanted $10 to go to McDonalds. BITCH PLEASE! And Shelia, you talking about protocol… I gotta go down on all of leadership first but you done already beat me to it and you still ain't got nowhere… ummm…. James and Michael… Ya'll commenting but ya'll on the low… Ya'll was in the bathroom last week busting each other asses open. Now leave me the fuck alone! I ain't nobody's hoe! So, don't speak on what you don't know about cause I know true shit on every last one of you. Fuck with me if you want to… I'll fuck yo whole life up! Ya'll shit true but mine ain't and ya'll coming for me… where they do that shit at…I'm beyond tired of the bullshit!"

Their jokes felt like painful blows stabbing me from behind but I refused to let the sting of it show. I choked down my emotions and sat there as if I was unbothered. It had become painfully obvious why another church member did what she did. Her name was Kelly. They did the same thing to her and she walked out of church, made her way to the bridge on I-45 and jumped! Her whole life outside the church had been hard. On top of that, she was forced to come to church every day to endure more of the same hell. She'd had about all she could take. She dove face first and plummeted 36 feet, till she become one with the ground below. You would have thought something like this would have made an impact on people, but no one cared. No one but me. Although, I wondered if the real reason I cared was because I wished it was me that died that day instead of her.

I thought cutting myself would make me immune to the pain's others caused, but it didn't. The cuts got deeper and deeper in non-visible places, but I still felt the hurt inside. I felt like hot garbage baking under the summer sun. Despair came with every breath I took as I faced the whispers and stares generated from the rumors. The gossip had condemned me before a real crime could even be committed. Every day I was living in hell and then I had to go to church. The one place where a person is supposed to go to get free. I would leave feeling more weighed down than I did before I went in. I had to listen to the accusations, lies, and comments of condemnation being passed down on me. My insecurities and feelings of worthlessness mounted up in me, growing larger than the brokenness, bitterness, and pain that already existed.

Chapter 18

One night I tied a rope to a hook hanging from the ceiling. I placed the other end around my neck and jumped. The rope snapped before the leap could kill me! I woke up with bruises around my neck and a sore throat. It felt like six full grown elephants were sitting on my shoulders. That heaviness weighed on me something fierce. Devastated that my attempt had failed, I sat down and began making a list of 101 ways to commit suicide. My plan was to try them all until I found one that worked. I climbed up on the roof of the apartment building and jumped... only to break my ankle!

I stole and collected every prescription pill bottle I could get my hands on. I poured all the pills into a bowl, mixed them around and swallowed them by the handful. I even chased them with vodka... only to wake up in a hospital bed! Robin found my body on the floor surrounded by the empty pill bottles and called 911. They got me to the hospital in enough time to pump my stomach. I woke up feeling like someone had both hands on my insides wringing my guts like a wet towel. One hand going in one direction, the other hand going in the opposite direction, twisting tighter and tighter. But... I was still alive!

Mandated into immediate counseling, I was kicked out after being told they didn't have the services necessary to help me. All they could offer was a prayer that I got help somewhere. I left, got in my car and stepped on the gas. The last thing I remembered before losing consciousness was looking at my speedometer reach 101 mph. This was the fastest I'd ever gone. Aiming for the tree in front of me, I wrapped my car around it… only to walk away with a few minor cuts! FUUUCK! Death keeps rejecting me!

I wondered if staying with Robin and Mitchell would've been a whole lot easier than trying to break free. I didn't know what was more damaging… the things done to me or the lies spread about me. Already feeling broken, shattered and hurt, depression reared its ugly head and it ran deep. Most days, the words people said to me cut just as deep as the knives, finger nail files and scissors ever did. I couldn't get past the fact that these were the ones who were supposed to love me. The very ones who were still telling me they loved me even in the midst of all of that. I wished for nothing more than to be dead, but it would have just given them something else to talk about. Perhaps it might've even given them another laugh at my expense.

Man God,

Death won't take me… You apparently can't stand me. What did I do to either of you? Are you even real? Because I can't feel you at all. I can't see you in the people I'm looking at. They all talk about you like you're the greatest thing but all I keep finding is the corruptness within the pews. This love has so many stipulations, restrictions, and requirements. I'm not sure if I can measure up anymore. My heart doesn't even want to. Have I found you and this is who you are?

Again, I left the church. I started going back to the new church, New Life Temple of the First Born C.M.E. Shortly after returning there, I woke up to Mitchell and Robin standing at the foot of my bed, watching me. It scared the hell out of me!

"You sleep too hard. We been watching you for a while. You

BETTER stay yo muthafucking ass away from that church! This gone be the last time I tell yo little dumb ass that!" He said.

My instincts told me to run… to get away from them, but there was nowhere to go. It was only one exit to this small turquoise room and I had to pass them both to get to it. I thought about taking my chances but my nerves kept me grounded. On the inside I could feel myself begin to panic, but as fast as it started to rise up I told myself to "bitch up" and take whatever was about to happen. I braced myself.

I learned a long time ago that people like that got off on seeing your fear and your tears. There was a power they got from it and I refused to give them that satisfaction of knowing they were mentally and physically wearing me down. At the time my internal battle was a lot worse than this one war they declared on me. As I sat there I kept repeating to myself don't give up, hang in there, it's gone be ok. I probably should have been more scared than I was, but right now I was more nervous than anything else. I didn't know what they were going to do. I still wasn't going to stay away from the church.

The more I looked at them the more I could see my uncle, Matthew and J.C. all wrapped up in Mitchell. I didn't think anything good ever lied in him. I even started to notice that Tiffany and Robin had some similarities. They both gained my trust under false pretenses. I felt like I had been cursed and no matter how hard I tried to break free I couldn't and because of it I now lived in this dark place where I no longer cared how much they hurt me. I wasn't surprised by it. I expected it but refused to give them the satisfaction of seeing me break. I had a tug-of-war of emotions going on inside me. Part of me refused to submit in defeat to them but the other part of me wanted to give up and die so, I wished and prayed that instead of tormenting me they would just kill me and get it over with. Either way I didn't get a lot of sleep for months after that. I waited for him to appear at the foot of my bed again and finally I got what I was waiting for.

The next time I woke up to my blanket over my head, being pressed down on my face. I couldn't breathe. Fear consumed me… I began to panic and struggle to get free. As tears ran down my face I knew it was him. I could feel the veins bulging out the back of his hand as he pressed down. I tried to turn my head to get air. I pushed and pulled at it trying to create an air pocket in the cover so I could breathe. I clawed and pulled at his hands, hoping it would loosen his grip, but he squeezed it tighter and pushed harder. The more I fought to create an air pocket to breathe the faster my heart pounded. I felt myself becoming light headed. I heard a voice in my head say, "he wants you dead so give him what he wants… play dead".

That's when I finally got one. The air pocket I had exhaustingly tried to create. I held what little breath I could manage to suck in and stopped moving. He let go. Though I was extremely light headed I laid motionless with my eyes open, barely letting breaths in or out. He pulled the cover down, looked at me, walked towards the door, cut the light out and closed the door behind him. As soon as the light went off I started trying to breathe regularly again. I coughed into my pillow while trying desperately not to be heard. Tears flowed nonstop. With my head pounding, thoughts racing and hands shaking, pains shot through my body! Shallowly breathing, I heard that same voice in my head telling me "Take deep breaths. Calm down. You're alright…" I laid there in disbelief as I tried to pull myself together. He thought he killed me!

The next morning, I walked out my room into the living room. There she was, sitting on the tan microfiber couch, wrapped in a blue and white checker patterned fleece blanket. Her mouth fell open, her face went pale, and she looked as if she had seen a ghost! I asked her "why she let him in my room"

"I didn't know he was in there" She replied.

I knew she was lying. She knew when he went to the bathroom and stopped pissing. She knew how many times he shook his dick before he put it back in his pants! She knew how many times he chewed his food before he swallowed. She knew his every move, even when they were in separate houses. So she damn sure knew he was in my room and what he was up to. In that moment I'm not sure what was raging in me more, the hurt or the anger. She was supposed to be my best friend. I trusted her! My ride or die and she let him kill me… or so she thought. I spent many days after that silently sobbing in that same pillow.

I was always looking over my shoulder because I never know when one of them was going to appear. They did more than show up at random hours of the night in my room. One Thursday I was leaving the house, heading up to my weekly meeting. I made it to the corner where I was confronted by a group of women from the church. One of them spoke up and asked, "Didn't Mitchell tell you to stay away from that muthafucking church?" I ignored her and continued walking. They surrounded me.

"So you gon' act like you don't hear me talking to you?" D'Aja spoke again.

"I don't give a fuck what he told me…Mitchell don't run me!"

D'Aja was another one of his girlfriends. She was "dickmatized" and would kiss the ground he walked on if he commanded her to, but I didn't realize he had so many. All of them were running for the same position… to replace his wife and become first lady! They wanted the prestige, power, and recognition that came along with being the first lady and was willing to do anything that made themselves look pleasing in his sight. His words were law so, if he spoke it, it was done.

"See the problem with bitches like you is you don't recognize a good thing when you see one. So you start doing dumb shit that could fuck it up for the rest of us. If we got to beat cha ass to get it through yo fucking head that you ain't going nowhere because you too much of a liability, then that's what the fuck we gone do to keep yo mouth closed!"

I looked around and saw in their faces the anger building up inside of them. I disconnected myself from my emotions, braced myself for the fight and became numb inside. I challenged them.

"Talk is cheap and ain't none of you sorry bitches gone stop me so do what you gone do!"

She punched me right in the face. When the first fist was thrown I told myself "Bitch you bet not waiver or fall." I went into a zone as we fought. It was like a movie playing out in front of me. All the hurt I had endured channeled a strength I didn't know I had. It was six of them on me and I was handling myself well. I was fighting to kill! As I moved forward they'd step back. I was purposely leading them into traffic, hoping a car would be going too fast to stop and hit us all. One by one I would grab a chick and keep swinging, non-stop. Knocking them into cars, pushing them into the building behind us… I refused to let any of these sorry bitches take me down. One of them kept grabbing me trying to pull me to the ground so they could stomp me. They were older than me so I could tell I was starting to wear them out. Instead of all together, they started coming in waves which made things easier for me. I felt my hair being wrapped around her hand. My neck snapped and pain shot through me in different directions as she yanked my hair, trying to get me on the ground. I think I thought I was a ninja for a minute!

Since she was a lot taller than me I ran up her body, wrapped my legs around her neck and squeezed my thighs as tight as I could. She let my hair go as I climbed, scared of what I was about to do. She bit down on my legs trying to get me to release her. When she let go to take a breath, I grabbed the upper part of her mouth and pulled with everything I had. It felt like she was trying to eat me alive but I didn't care! As she fell to the ground I jumped off so I wouldn't fall too! I went on to the next one. We shut down Salem Court fighting that day! There were moments in that fight where I knew one wrong move could get me killed. Had I hit that ground they would've stomped me. Though I wanted to die and was fixated on it, I refused to allow them bitches to take me out!

Someone had apparently called the police. The sound of the sirens in the distance broke up the fight. As everyone began to limp and run in different directions towards their cars, I looked up to see Robin standing on the top porch. She was on the phone watching the whole thing! I knew she was talking to Mitchell and telling him everything. She looked at me and smiled. I rolled my eyes and began heading towards the church.

During the fight some ladies that went to New Life ran in to tell Pastor Monica Watson, the head pastor, about the fight that was taking place up the street! She felt like it was me and called my phone. It was in my pocket and I had no idea it had answered. She actually heard what was going on! She started to pray and sent some of the women to find me and bring me back to her. One of them picked me up a few blocks away. As soon I walked in the door, people tried to touch me and see about me. I moved away from them so they couldn't. As long as no one touched me I was fine. I stayed put together well, but as soon as she grabbed me and hugged me all I could do was cry. They stood around us rubbing my back as I sobbed. My shirt was hiked up so, one of the ladies saw the cut down my back and the bruises. She whispered in the pastor's ear. She just held me tightly. Then, we walked into her office and I told her everything.

"Do you want me to go talk to him? Because I don't have a problem confronting him!"

"NO, Please DON'T!" I broke down crying even harder. "I know what they're capable of and I don't want to feel responsible for anything happening to you because of me. I wouldn't be able to handle that guilt."

"You don't have to worry about me… I got me and God got me. Mitchell and I can talk Pastor to Pastor."

"No, just let it go. I'm only telling you so if something happens and you stop seeing me and hearing from me, you'll know why." She prayed for me then hugged me for what seemed like forever. It was the first time I felt a little peace on the inside.

"Listen to me baby… you need to get out that house and get away from them. Otherwise, they are going to kill you. Do you have anywhere else you can stay?"

"No, not right now." I couldn't think of anywhere. I had family but none of us were close. I hadn't really seen or talked to any of them since the funeral.

"Are you working? What are you doing for money?"

"Not much anymore. I got let go from one job and I wasn't there long enough to collect unemployment. On the other job I'm barely working. It's part time… four hours a week. They usually put me on the schedule two weeks out of the month. It's hard but I'm making it".

"It's cold outside. Why do you keep wearing that hoodie?"

"Because I don't have a winter coat. This is all I have."

"I can't do much at the moment but what I can do I will. I'm going to put you on a $25 a week allowance to help you out until you get back on your feet".

"Thank you, I appreciate it. Every little bit helps."

"Hang in their sweetie. Don't give up."

I did my best to stretch that $25 like it was $100, to get both food and personal needs. If I had a little left over I would save it. I was saving up to buy a winter coat. The one I wanted was in a little shop in Clifton Park. It was on sale for $20. Sometimes I stole my personal needs just to make sure I had enough to last and so I could get one step closer to getting my coat. The temperatures were dropping more and more each day. After a few months I finally had enough money saved. I walked 22 blocks to Southside Fashion in Clifton Park. I couldn't afford to catch the bus and get the coat so I had to make a decision.

The cold winds slapped my face so hard it felt like someone was throwing bags of ice cubes at me the entire time. My hands were going numb so I kept blowing on them as I walked to get the feeling in them again. When I walked into the store a blast of heat hit me so hard I thought I was melting. It felt great! I was elated to see the store still had a sale on. I walked around looking at all the racks, trying to decide which one I wanted. Finally, I came across this thick black fur down coat, lined with fleece on the inside. The hood was lined as well. I tried it on and knew instantly it was for me. I walked to the register and put the coat and everything I had on the counter. My total came to $22.34. I forgot about the tax! I almost fainted as I stared at the register. I walked all the way up here in the cold for nothing! Disappointed, I told the cashier to cancel my order and took my money off the counter.

"What's wrong? The coat rung up and all your excitement left."

"I've been saving for the past few months just to come up here and get a coat. I walked all the way here from 45th and

Salem Court just to get it and I still don't have enough."

"Damn! That's far as hell! Why did you walk?" He asked.

"Yea, I know… but I couldn't afford to catch the bus and get the coat."

"I can't let you leave out of here with nothing. Give me $15 and the coat is yours".

"Seriously!" I shouted with a new rush of excitement. I couldn't wait to put my new coat on! I felt so proud.

"Yes, seriously."

"Oh my God! Thank you so much! I'm starving! Now I have enough left over to go across the street to McDonalds and get a dollar sandwich plus catch the bus back home. You don't know what a blessing you've been! Thank you so so much!"

I couldn't wait to go to my next meeting with my new coat on and tell her what happened. Those Thursday meetings were the highlight of my week. It was my moment of safety and peace in the midst of all the chaos.

I can't even count how many times I'd be walking up or down Burk Road or Salem Court and he would pull up on me. He'd say "didn't I tell you to stay away from that church?" How many times I had to fight my way free… Sometimes, it felt like the church was a cult. It was easy to get in but there was no way out. I was in way too deep with Mitchell and Robin long before I realized exactly what it was I was into. She had my heart because she was there to help me through a whole lot of stuff before things got bad. He had my mind because after a while, I remained in a constant state of fear. They had so much of me that I had none.

Robin was like Dr. Jekyll and Mrs. Hyde. I never knew which one I was gon' get but, I couldn't handle any more heartache. The amount of pain I could absorb had reached its limit. I had finally landed a decent job at First United National Bank, so I took my first check and got an apartment as far away from everybody as I could get. I was able to get a car. I packed what little I had and left while Robin was at Mitchell's house. As I was leaving I tried to take Carla with me, but she was too scared to go. I begged her to run with me but she didn't. I told her I would protect her but she wouldn't listen.

She stayed behind and replaced me with Mitchell and Robin. I felt so guilty because I knew the hell and fear she was living in and I couldn't do anything about it. She blamed me for where she was. She said she only got involved with them so she could be closer to me. Now she was dying on the inside and I abandoned her. That guilt never left me but I couldn't go back to try to save her without getting caught myself. Every so often, I would see her and try to convince her to come home with me but she wouldn't do it. My apartment was bare but I didn't care. It was mine and we could share my floor together. I started furnishing it little by little. I was free but I wasn't completely safe. The guilt behind leaving my best friend in a corrupt world of hell was eating at me. My drinking had gotten worse because only part of my environment changed. I still needed an escape from my reality. Even when I wasn't drunk I wanted to be.

Chapter 19

Just before summer I started kicking it with Kesha, Crystal, and Will… some folks I knew from back in the day. We smoked and drank all the time. One night I was high and drunk and knew I had no business behind the wheel. I had been drinking since the day before but we were hungry and I was the soberest out of everyone! None of the restaurants near us were open so we decided to drive across town. I hopped on the highway to get there quicker. Windows down, cool breeze blowing, music blaring, heads bobbing… we were having a blast! That was till I slammed on the breaks and came to a complete stop in the middle of the highway! I saw someone walking across the road and I almost hit them! I started screaming for them to get out the way. Everyone in the car was scared and praying.

"Girl ain't nobody in the middle of the highway! Man, you fucking up my high!"

"Yes it was! I saw them walking!"

"No… you just real fucked up and you seeing shit!"

"I really saw them! I'm so serious…"

"Move, so I can drive. Yo ass gone either get us arrested or killed!"

It scared me shitless. When the next set of cars passed we hopped out the car, ran to the other side and got back in. I got in the passenger's seat and Kesha drove us to get food and back home. The whole ride I thought my heart was gone jump out my chest! I was so scared my hands were shaking. I kept taking deep breaths to try to calm down.

Dear God,

If you can hear me I need you to keep the people off the road and let us make it back safely. Don't let us hurt nobody. In Jesus name.

Amen

I never picked up another set of keys intoxicated. It took me a while to recover from that night and trust myself behind the wheel of a vehicle again.

By April of the following year, I had started dating this girl named Trina. We sang in the same choir at one of the churches I used to attend. I didn't really know how to love her because I didn't know how to love myself, but I thought I did. She would call my name...

"Karen! I love you..."

"Ok, thank you... It's nice to know you feel that way". I'd reply.

See... love cost too much and was no longer a word in my vocabulary. So moving forward, every time I heard those three words, that was my response. I could tell by the look on her face that it hurt her feelings, but I didn't care. I was at war with myself and though I craved a hug I was terrified of a touch. I wanted no parts of love. I'd had enough of it and been hurt too bad from it, but I still wanted somebody to love me. The only problem was that nobody was giving out hugs for free. The touch that I so needed would cost too much. I was in a constant war with my emotions and it caused me and Trina to fight all the time.

It was in dating her that I realized just how crazy I had actually become. In the beginning our relationship was really good. Then she started bringing this new friend around named Shelly. She used to say they were just friends but in my eyesight, they were way too friendly. Things just weren't adding up. I felt I was being played, but every time I confronted her and asked if they were more than just friends, she denied it. We constantly fought and argued about it. Whenever I brought the subject up she would hit me but come back later and apologize. She said I just pushed her to her limit. Little did she know she was pushing me to mine too.

I was at a point where no one else was going to manipulate my feelings and play with my heart strings. There was an anger in me that I never really noticed was there till her. But, the word disgusted didn't even begin to describe what was going on inside me. I was so tired of people doing and saying whatever they wanted to me and expecting me to just accept it. I was done being a punching bag and a door mat. My gut told me "don't trust her… she's cheating!" Though I couldn't prove it, I was fed up.

We had a date scheduled to try to repair our relationship, but she didn't show up. I called myself getting out the house to clear my head and ran into Shelly.

"Heeeey Girl! Don't you look lonely"

"Have you seen Trina?"

"Yea she at my house in the bed waiting on me to get back". I could feel my fists clinching as I stared at her. I noticed she had bottles of caramel, chocolate and whip cream in her hands.

"Oh Really? Ok…"

"Yep you can come join us if you want" she laughed as I walked off.

When Trina finally came home she apologized. She said she was with Shelly and they lost track of time. So, again we were fighting like crazy. Glass shattering, hair pulling, fists swinging, cussing and rolling around the floor fighting. I meant it when I said I'd had all I could take! She left and I followed her. She went right back to Shelly's house. As soon as Shelly opened the door she kissed her and they walked in the house. I waited outside. My mind raced and I began to have a conversation out loud with myself.

Everybody was gone learn that day… "Never fuck over a person that has a set of keys to your car!"

It was a hot summer night. I went to the gas station and filled up my gas can. I moved the car and poured the gas all over the inside. When the sun rose, it baked it in the rest of the way. I was patient when it came to getting even. I was still talking to myself.

"Oh! You wanna hit me? Well, you hit me and hurt me for the last time! Let's see if the chick you laid up with right now is gone take care of you the same way I do!"

I walked up to the side of the house and saw them making love. That pissed me off even more!

"oh ok. I see you. I got you though" I said.

I went back to the car and poured even more gasoline all over the interior and exterior of the car. I waited for it to dry before I made my next move. Once it dried I called her phone and told her to come home. I laid low and watched as they left the house. Smiling and walking to the car like they got away with something, life was great for them. I continued to watch them. With confused looks on their faces, they searched the car trying to figure out where the gas smell was coming from. I heard Shelly as she suggested to Trina that maybe she had a gas leak. I popped up in front of the car with a lit match in my hand.

"See… I decided to get out the house to get some air and clear my head. I ran into your new chick and followed her home after she and I talked. I looked in the window as you fucked her. I can't believe you had the nerve to hit me when I addressed you. But, that's ok cause that's gone be the last time. Yea, you smell that don't you? It's not a gas leak. It's me…"

Every time she'd unlock the doors to get out I'd hit the switch to lock them back. She'd try to push the door open I'd push it closed. The look on their faces was priceless!

"Are you feeling lucky?" I asked. The look of terror in their eyes was fascinating to me as they choked from the fumes. "Ya'll gone learn one way or the other to quit fucking with me! Gloves off! I'm done playing nice. The hell with all ya'll!"

I threw the match at the car and it instantly went up in flames. I walked through the alley to my car and drove away. I saw her in my rear-view mirror. Damn! Too bad they made it, I thought. I figured maybe being alone was the best method for me because obviously, none of my relationships were working out.

I spent many days sitting in the window watching the clouds roll by and trying to figure out my life. Why did it seem like I was always fighting? I was fighting to live, fighting to survive, fighting to belong, fighting to be loved, fighting to find Jesus. It was a physical fight, a mental fight, a spiritual fight. I was just fighting and I was sick of it. I just wanted to belong. So, after a few years of rejecting love and swearing off church, I decided I'd give the whole religious thing another try. Plus, all my friends where "spiritual" and I was the odd man out. I needed to belong somewhere. I stood out no matter where I went and I wanted company.

My friends spent their days either working or at church. I wanted someone to talk to besides myself. I was lonely and part of me wanted to believe that there was a chance I could still find God. I wanted so badly to believe that I was a part of something. I wanted more than anything to believe that someone truly loved me without me having to sacrifice anything for it. A part of me wanted to believe that out of everything I experienced, there was still a piece of me somewhere that was a little loveable. Once again, I found myself following along with the pack. I joined yet another church. Not because it was some mighty move of God or anything, but because it's where all my friends were. I wanted to be with somebody.

It was there that I met Minister Christian Michaelson. Though I couldn't stand people with a title and never desired nor saw myself as qualified to be a first lady he had my attention. I fantasized about our future together long before we ever got serious with one another. Christian was 6'4, built just right, dark chocolate, preppy with a touch of thug handsome man. His slightly nerdy flare mentally intrigued me and that's the part of him I adored the most. We met during a revival and hit it off instantly. I especially loved the fact that we could talk openly and freely, with no judgement. There was an ice cream parlor around the corner from the church. We'd meet there a couple nights a week to discuss life over cups of pistachio almond and butter pecan ice cream into the wee hours of the night. We talked about our likes, dislikes, dreams, inspirations, relationships with God, what we wanted our futures to look like, family, news, and more. There weren't many people that could stimulate me mentally but he could. He accepted me with my past and I had a really crazy past. I accepted him for his too. I believed everything he told me. I mean… why lie when we're so open with each other?

The day before we were to meet up again, he found out he was going to be an uncle. He was so happy!

"Guess what?"

"I'm going to be an uncle. My sister in law's finally pregnant!"

"Awww that's awesome. How far is she?"

"I don't know yet, but I hope it's a boy."

"So kids is something we haven't discussed yet. Do you want to be a father?"

"OH NNNNNOOOOOO. I like kids but I want to be able to return them when I'm ready. I'd rather travel and see the world instead of staying in one place raising a child. What about you? Do you want kids?"

"Being a mother used to be one of my dreams but life had something different in store for me. I found out a few years ago that I can't have children"

"Oh I'm sorry to hear that…"

"It's ok life goes on… Sometimes you just got to roll with the punches and keep moving."

"Well now we have something else we can share together…"

"What's that?"

"No Children!" We laughed, shifted the conversation in a different direction and continued talking.

Chapter 20

In my eyes, he was my God send. He was the perfect gentlemen. He caters to me, opens doors, the works. At first, we talked all day and when we weren't talking we were texting. When our work schedules got ridiculously busy we still made it a point to call and text periodically throughout the day. We just wanted to let each other know we were thinking about them. Life was great! We were riding the love train, moving full speed ahead and planning our life together. Within 5 months of us dating we were engaged!

That's where we went wrong. When I accepted the proposal, I was ecstatic. I didn't think I was worthy of anyone loving me let alone loving me enough to propose but here I was on the verge of getting married! Or, so I thought anyway. Less than 24 hours after I said yes, our relationship changed. I began to see a different man. It felt like I went to sleep with one person and woke up to someone completely different. I couldn't stand this new dude I was with. He got on my nerves! He too just became another story in my life. This is one of those times where I just had to laugh to keep from crying.

Every time I turned around we were arguing. If it wasn't one thing it was another. Half of our arguments I didn't understand. It seemed like he was purposely doing stuff to get under my skin until I was pissed off. He'd let things escalate then say, "I was just playing". I didn't see the humor in anything though. I wondered if maybe my life had just caused me to be too serious of a person or if this was something I needed to pay attention to. I had this deep-rooted feeling that he was playing with my head. Though I kept telling myself I was wrong, I still couldn't figure out why we were fighting like sworn enemies.

Even if our day started out good, before long it went to hell in a hand basket! Part of me thought he was doing it on purpose to get away from me. Then the other side of me thought it might just be something in me that caused it. Though I battled with myself I never told him. I just sat back and watched. During our good times he would randomly say things…

"So, you ready to have my baby? I want kids."

"Are you being serious right now?"

"Yea, can't you see that little face that look like us running around here?" I'd just stand there looking at him like he was stupid.

"How is that gon' happen? Who having it? Do you have a surrogate in mind you ain't told me about?"

"Naw you gone have it. Sarah couldn't have a baby but God gave her one. He gone give us one too?"

"Oh ok… well you keep waiting on it and let me know how that works out for you."

"See that's the shit I be talking about right there! I'm trying to lead us in faith and you so nonchalant."

"Well what you want me to do? Get excited and start jumping up and down about an idea of something I came to terms with and accepted wasn't a part of my reality a long time ago? Just because now you wavering between wanting to be a daddy and not wanting to be one…?"

"I'm trying to build us and you just refuse to work with me. Everything I say you got a response for when all I need you to do is follow along. DAMN! You getting on my nerves!"

"Yea I'm going to have a response especially when the shit doesn't make sense! And hell… the feeling is mutual. This shit right here is the shit I don't understand. We've had countless conversations about children long before we ever got engaged and we have been on one accord this whole time. Now all of a sudden you want kids and I'm supposed to get all excited until two days from now when you don't want them no more! Every time I turn around it seem like you're lookin' for a reason for us to argue. I don't know what you did with the man I fell in love with but I wish you'd hurry up and find him cause I can't fucking stand you! You wearin' my damn nerves out! All day… Every day…. Every time I turn around it's something else. I'm drained and exhausted from it all".

Arguing with him became a full-time job that I didn't apply for. I was so over the arguing. Thinking I was doing right, I got to a point where in the middle of us arguing I would just stop mid-sentence and tune him out. I couldn't take all the going back and forth. It was annoying me so bad it made my skin crawl. The arguing soon started to escalate quicker than our relationship did. In the middle of one of our arguments he hit me upside my head. Initially, it took me by surprise. It took my brain a few minutes to really register that this just happened. I couldn't believe I had just got hit. "Did this muthafucker just hit me?" I said out loud. I'm arguing with self yet, still standing there confused as to what actually just took place. I looked at him

"Have you lost your fucking mind?"

"Have you?" he replied.

"Hell, I'm about to lose it right along with you. I can't believe you just hit me!"

"I didn't hit you. I laid hands on you in the name of Jesus. It's what I do…"

"Yup! Well if that's the case, Jesus gon' cause you to have a well whooped ass! Cause anytime my head snaps back, you didn't just lay hands muthafucker! You hit me! So how about going forward you don't do either".

He stormed out but at that point I could care less about his attitude. I guess I should've reacted more than just verbally then because it continued to happen more often. Because of my past I could handle being hit almost anywhere on my body. I only partially cared about that. But my face was completely off limits! Hitting me in my face was a trigger for me and today he pulled my trigger. I had reached my wits end with this relationship but I refused to give up. I was praying for better days to come back. I kept telling myself that all relationships go through dark periods. I justified his actions.

Since he was a minister, maybe he was going through a difficult time spiritually and just wasn't discussing it. I couldn't for the life of me figure out what happened to the man I loved and where this one came from. I felt like I was alone in my relationship. I noticed I was getting more and more infuriated. The hits and the arguments kept coming until finally I exploded. I erupted to the point where my neighbors were nervous. Prior to this moment, they never heard or saw me unless they stopped me on my way into the house and decided to have a conversation. However, on this particular day, in the middle of one of our arguments he shouts

"I'm so sick of you! I thought I would be able to change you and teach you how to be a woman, but I see now I was wrong. I don't have time to raise you!"

"Raise me... Raise me? I've already been raised! I was a grown ass woman long before you met me and I'll be a grown ass woman when you leave! Since we venting... by all means allow me! I feel like I'm supposed to be the Bitch in this relationship but my dick hang so low I got scrapes across the tip from it hitting the ground! I'm looking around trying to figure out where the fuck yours at!"

Before I knew it, my head snapped back so hard I strained a muscle in my neck and the knife in my hand was going for his chest. I couldn't stop myself. It was like I was standing outside my own body watching all of this happen and I couldn't control it. My face was red, my feelings were hurt, I was extremely pissed, and I could taste the bitterness of my anger in the back of my throat. It went down in my house that day! In the midst of us fighting there was a knock on the door. I opened it two police officers standing in front of me and my heart dropped.

"Good evening ma'am may we come in".

Fuck me running! Now I'm about to go to jail and I have to work tomorrow! Tears fell from my eyes as I stepped aside. My neighbors had never heard me yelling, cussing, and objects breaking so when they did they called the police. I felt humiliated.

They split us up and talked to us separately. The male officer took him outside and as they were leaving out Christian tells the officer

"Sorry for the disturbance sir she was just having a temper tantrum"

"A temper tantrum…" I proceeded to follow them out to see what more he had to say. She rested her hand on my arm and guided me back into the dining room.

"So what's really going on here?" I told her everything… the truth…

"Look, I can't tell you how to live your life but I can tell you that true love will communicate not abuse and yes, it is laying hands just not the ones its being portrayed as. Are you really that desperate for someone to love you that you're willing to accept anything? You do know that if this is what's it's like in the engagement phase it's not going to get better once you say I DO. You two might be better off apart".

"But maybe it can change back. He's not the man I fell for."

"Yes he is he just showed you the parts of him he wanted you to see and now you're learning the rest of him"

"How long have you been together?"

"5 months" her mouth dropped, eyes bulged, and she let out a big sigh

"Ummm… 5 months is not long enough to know the depths of anyone". She was right but my heart needed to make this relationship work. We continued to talk until her partner came back in the house. They spoke with each other then he walked over to me.

"Ma'am I sent him home. We agreed that the two of you need some time apart. I suggest you take it because if we are called back here again the next time one or both of you will be arrested" I felt relieved.

Once the police left, my neighbor that stayed diagonally from me knocked on my door to see if I was ok.

We didn't talk for a couple of days and I was perfectly ok with that. Until he finally reached out to me to apologize and talk. Of course, I forgave him and things went back to how they originally were for about 3 weeks.

Chapter 21

One night as we sat watching a movie, a conversation arose based off of what we were looking at. In the movie the guy walked in on his girl having sex with another woman.

"See it don't pay to cheat you gone eventually get caught"

"Eating ain't cheating"

"Excuse me!"

"Eating… Ain't… Cheating?"

"Please clarify because anything with someone other than the one you committed to is cheating"

"No, it's not! If you have sex with someone of the same sex it's not cheating. It's only cheating if you have sex with someone of the opposite sex".

Out of curiosity I decide to keep it going. I wanted to know where and how far this conversation could go. The moment he told me "eating ain't cheating" all kind of red flags went up. Normally I would have ignored the red flags but this one I just couldn't let go.

"Ok let me ask you this... If you walked in the house and saw me having sex with another woman you'd be ok with that?"

"Yea! I'd probably watch for a little bit then go in another part of the house until you're finished. I'd ask you if it was good and if you enjoyed yourself. That would be the end of it."

"Wait… WHAT? You gotta be shittin me… this can't be for

real" I couldn't wrap my mind around this conversation.

"No, seriously I would…"

"Ok so let me ask you this then…" Now, where this question came from I don't know. It popped into my head and flew out my mouth.

"So, if I walked in and you had another man's dick in yo mouth, I'm supposed to be ok with it?"

"Yes! Because it's only cheating if it's the opposite sex!"

"You got me ALL the way Fucked Up if you think I'm gone be ok with that bullshit! If I walk in the house and you fucking another man, they gone have to bury me under the jail cause I'm killing yo ass and him too! As a woman… if you fucking another woman that's one thing. I'd feel like, ok I need to step my game up. A woman can compete with another woman all day long… but a man? A man! I can't compete with that shit because he will forever have something that I don't have. He'll be able to touch you and reach you on levels that I can never get to because I'm not where your interests lie. So… do men turn you on?"

To me, the question seemed valid based off the direction this conversation went in. Since the door was opened why not walk my little ass right on through it! I want to know exactly what I'm getting myself into. I don't do surprises. Tell me what I'm facing up front and let me decide if that's a door I want to walk through. However, instead of answering the question he got upset and walked into another room. I followed him…

"Oh hell naw! You're not getting' out this conversation that easy".

"Damn… gone cause you starting shit!"

"Naw I didn't start it but I bet I sure as hell finish it! That was a yes or no question"

By now, I've noticed that anytime he doesn't want to respond to me he starts an argument or hits me upside my head, like its gone make me forget what we were talking about. Since he knows my triggers he tries to use it to his advantage. Normally it would work but this time I ain't going. In not answering the question at all, you just answered it.

"Fuck this arguing over nothing! Answer me. Do men turn you on? What's the likelihood of this scenario playing out in real life?"

"Damn get off the subject... It's over with now... See man... you tripping! I've been delivered!"

"Well how deep into your deliverance are you? Are you delivered like... back in the closet, creeping on the down low delivered? Or like zero interest in men delivered? Which end of the scale we talkin' about here?" I believe in giving people the benefit of the doubt but as bad as I wanted to believe in him, every fiber of my being told me to continue to push the envelope for answers. So I did!

His hand glided up the back of my head, jerking it forward.

"Just drop the fucking subject... DAMN!" He yelled.

I picked up a chair and threw it at him. As it hit him he became more pissed off.

"Just answer the fucking question... DAMN! Do you like CLITS or DICKS!? BITCH! What's your FUCKING preference? See 'No' should've been your first response. So since you keep tryna ignore me, let me rephrase my questions. Do you like busting asses or getting busted in the ass?"

He grabbed me, pushing me backwards into the bedroom where he threw me across the bed. I was shocked! I didn't know he had that much strength in him.

"JUST MOVE THE FUCK ON AND LET IT GO... AS

LONG AS YOU STAY IN YO LANE AND PLAY YO FUCKING ROLE YOU AINT GOT SHIT TO WORRY ABOUT!!!!" He screamed.

Though everything in me told me to walk away from the relationship, I still justified everything he said. It was toxic yet I stayed. Through every out of line, disrespectful, and completely out of order comment he made, I stayed. After every hit he threw I stayed. I really wanted to make it work. I wanted my relationship to be real and to last for once. I wanted to believe he was REALLY delivered so that somebody could love me and just choose me for a change. I convinced myself that maybe this was a test from God. Maybe it was God's way of showing me that my mouth and my attitude needed a whole lot of work. That maybe, just maybe this was somehow preparing me to be a better wife. So, I stayed.

I let it go verbally but not mentally. The warning signs were always there. I just came up with excuses for it. Stuff that had been going on all throughout the relationship that I noticed but chose to overlook, was starting to come back to mind. Things like… if we were out in public he would hold my hand and act like we were this beautiful loving couple. But, behind closed doors he wouldn't touch me at all. No hand holding, no hugging, no kiss on the cheek… nothing, unless I said something. Then he would do it like it was a pacifier. When I brought it up he'd say it was because of him being a preacher. He didn't want to be tempted in any kind of way because he was addicted to sex in the past. I thought, ok I can respect that. Then, I brought up the fact that he knew about all my friends and had talked to them, yet I never met any of his. So, he took me around the city and introduced me to all his friends. Not ONE of them was straight!!!!!!!

I wasn't sure what to think at that moment or what I was getting myself into. My heart wanted so bad to believe everything he told me. For a little while I did. But, my mind wouldn't rest. It was eating at me and before I knew it I started up again.

"SSSSOOOOOOO Inquiring minds want to know…"

"Whose mind is inquiring?" he asked.

"Hell, mine! I'm the one asking the question…" He just shook his head. "Why did it take you so long to say you weren't into men?"

"Look! I told you my point of view and now it's an issue. Now you judging me…"

"I'm not judging anything but I want the cards on the table. Let me know what I'm up against out the gate and let me decide if it's something I want to be a part of. Don't take my choice from me and put me in a situation where I've taken a life".

"I just believe what I believe and I think we should be able to do whatever we want with whoever we want. I believe we should have an open, but slightly closed relationship. All you have to do is play your role."

"My role? So, basically you want me to let you do whoever you gone do of the same sex, even though you don't like men and you're no longer gay… so I'll play the happy first lady role and accept it all."

"Oh! So, you do know your role after all…"

I didn't say a word after that. I was done and as soon as the conversation ended, that other man that I couldn't stand showed up and stayed. I was leaving Saturday anyway to go to Kentucky to see Stacy's new baby. It was a much needed break from my life. I didn't tell anyone about that conversation. We hadn't really spoken much the whole time I was gone until he called me out of the blue one day.

"Hey baby I just wanted to let you know that me and your

God sister April got into an argument at church because she started lying on me and being messy. She's tryna start up some drama". As long as I've known her she has been very blunt, straightforward and very opinionated. She shoots straight from the hip and hates, and I do mean HATES drama.

"What did she do?"

"You need to quit talking to her and stay away from her because she is messy as hell and she never used to be that way. I think it's because of the new people she hanging around with."

"Ok… so what did she do?"

"Baby, hold on. I have another call coming in. I need to grab this and I'll call you right back."

"Ok" I hung up the phone. Needless to say, I wasn't surprised when April called me a few minutes later to tell me what happened.

"Sis! You not gone beeeellliiieeevvve what I got to teeeellllllllllllllll you! Ok… so you know we had that three-day revival this past weekend…."

"Yea…"

"Well I brought my friend from work with me. As soon as Christian saw her he walked up to us and asked her what are we doing together. I said she's my friend from work. He looked at her and said, "what the fuck are you doing here?" She said she came for the service. So, I asked my home girl how she knew him. She said she used to be engaged to him!"

"Engaged? He didn't tell me he was engaged before."

"Girl Yes! And the stuff she told me… Hold on I'm about to call her because you got to hear it for yourself."

The phone rings and a woman with the sweetest voice answers. "Hello?"

"Hey Tina. I have my sister on the line. Tina… Karen, Karen… Tina."

"Nice to meet you."

"You too."

"So, I was told that you were engaged to my fiancé?"

"Yes I was. We dated for a few years before we got engaged."

"When did ya'll break up?"

"About 6 1/2 months ago. Why?" I didn't say anything

"Hello?"

"Yes I'm here…"

"Why? How long have ya'll been together"

"6 months"

"Why did ya'll break up?"

"I'm not sure you really want me to answer that. I'm not bitter or angry about anything anymore, but I'm not sure telling you is the best thing for your relationship. You should really talk to him about that."

"But I'm asking you. You're the one on the phone right now."

"My sister can handle it. You can tell her."

"You sure?"

"Yes" I answered

"Well everything in our relationship was great for the longest time. Then, one day everything changed. He became a totally different person. I didn't know him anymore. In the beginning, he was the sweetest man I had ever encountered but once we got engaged he became abusive. The final straw was when I came home and walked in on him having sex with another man. He got up, took my keys, told me he didn't want me anymore, said he was leaving me for the guy and put me out the house. Literally…he physically put me out the house. I never spoke to him again until the day I saw him at the church."

There was silence on the line. I was speechless because this sounded way too familiar.

"Hello. Are you still there?"

"Yes, I'm still here. I just…. Wow"

"Well if it helps at all, people change and that's just my story about what happened to me. He could be a different person now."

"Did you know in advance? Were there any warning signs?"

"Like I said before, I noticed that he had changed. He became distant and everything was an argument. He became a little abusive but nothing would've prepared me for what I walked into. Nothing…"

"Ok well thank you for answering my questions."

"You're welcome. If you need anything else just call."

"Ok"

As we were hanging up the phone Christian called. I didn't want to say anything right away. I wanted to wait till we were face to face. I was flying back in town today so we planned to get together later in the evening for dinner. When I heard the lock on my door turning I knew it was Christian coming in. I hung in there as long as I could until I just absolutely, positively could NOT take any more. As always, we were back to arguing and fighting over everything. We were no longer fighting with words because I'd taken as much as I could.

God,

I can't win for losing. He was supposed to be my break. He was supposed to be my knight in shining armor and he turned out to be my princess in a tiara! Come on now Jesus... can you PLEASE give a sister a break? What did I do to deserve this kind of treatment? Why are you torturing me? You see I'm failing miserably in life! At what point does it get easier? Since as far back as I can remember everything's been a struggle. At what point in walking with you does the struggling end? And if the struggling never stops then what's the purpose of being a Christian? Don't I deserve to smile instead of hurting all the time? Where is my happily ever after? Oh I forgot I don't even know if I'm walking with you. I don't know if you're really a good God or if you just as bad as your representatives. MAAAAN I'm sick of this...

I finally got to the point where I had given up on us. I walked into his house, gave him his ring back told him "I can't do all this anymore. I'm calling it quits" and walked back out the door. A few months later he was engaged to someone else and a year later they were married. I'm glad he found his happily ever after. I still didn't know if I would ever find mine.

Chapter 22

Since I couldn't find my knight in shining armor to rescue me I let liquor do it instead. I didn't need liquid courage… I needed strength! I felt like the church crippled me but I kept being drawn back to it looking to them to fix my broken pieces so that I could find my way to God. My bottle was my hope and my help to keep going. My mood was dependent upon what I was drinking. Tequila stirred up the anger and rage in me and it poured out onto whoever I was around. Vodka stirred up my emotions. I continuously cried and called and told everyone how much I loved them and how much they hurt me. Gin allowed my true feelings to spill out with no filters or sugar coating. Mixing them all together was my truth serum. Equally, they each were my best friends. I bothered no one. I stayed to myself and I loved it that way. I tried to be social with a few, but when I didn't want to be bothered I'd cut the music up. I'd act like it was so loud I couldn't hear my door then cut the phone off so you couldn't call me.

I enjoyed my misery in all the isolation but one day I decided to sit outside and enjoy the sunshine and the fresh air. I watched as Pastor Tobias Walker, who lived in my same apartment complex three buildings over, chased people around the parking lot reading bible passages. He would catch them while getting out of their cars and talk to them about Jesus. He'd try to get them to come to his church. Our neighbors would cuss him out, push him out the way, knock his bible out his hand and throw it across the parking lot! He'd yell "That's ok! You can throw the book but I know the word here and there." He would point to his head then place his hand on his heart. "As long as I got the word where it matters the most it don't matter what you do to the book." Everyday like clockwork he'd be out there in the parking lot.

People would see him coming, get back in their cars and speed off before he would run over to them. Occasionally, he'd even come out with a mic and a small speaker. He'd stand in the center of the parking lot quoting scriptures. It was always hilarious until you were the one not paying attention and got caught. I was intrigued by him because no matter how bad people treated him, he didn't give up. He acted as if it didn't even bother him. Sometimes I'd come out, sit on the steps and just watch him till he'd head in my direction trying to talk to me.

"Hey you… little lady. Hold on. Let me talk to you."

"Uh un… You can keep ya Jesus crap. I'll be entertained by it but I don't want to hear it. You can have it. I'm good." I'd say as I quickly headed for my door. I wouldn't come out the rest of the day. If I had to go out I'd take the long way to my apartment, just in case he was outside. My attempts at hiding out didn't matter because he watched what door I walked into. He would periodically knock on my door throughout the day or just hang around close by trying to catch me as soon as the door opened. Eventually he succeeded.

"Hey little lady just give me 5 minutes of your time and I promise I won't bother you again".

"UH What the hell do you want? Can't you tell I don't want to be bothered?"

"I want to you to come visit my church. It'll change your life"

"Church already changed my life. It chewed me up and spit me out"

"I'm sorry you had such an awful experience but I'm the pastor. I'm different and so is my church"

"You're really not but ok… A title doesn't make you different. Hell, everybody I encountered had a title"

"All I'm asking for is a chance"

"NO!"

For weeks he came back every day for those same 5 damn minutes until I gave in and went to visit his church. The service was live but it had no substance. I watched as people cried and ran around the church, but it all just looked like a really good show with no feeling. I've heard people say God can do anything, but I watched most of those people outside my window pimping, hoeing, hustling, cussing and fighting. The rest of them I drank with at the club. After we popped bottles two nights before now they were super saved just because it was Sunday! Still I sat there waiting and watching to see if I would feel something. I wondered if God would move for real. After the fifth offering I got up and left. That was about all I could tolerate. This church wasn't any different than the rest of em'! I could watch a good show on TV. Sitting in there was a waste of my time.

Joanna called me while I was on my way home to see how the service went. I laughed and told her to meet me at the house. I left the door unlocked for her. So, when I heard a knock at the door I yelled "it's open!"

"I'll be up in just a second. We have so much to talk about. Man it was so crazy. Get yourself a drink while you wait if you want one." I was shocked when I walked in my living room and saw Pastor Walker sitting on my couch. The sight of him stopped me dead in my tracks.

"What the hell you doing in my house?"

"You said to come in."

"I thought you were someone else."

"Why are you here? You don't have nothing better to do?" As I asked the question, Joanna walked in.

"Well I came by to talk to you. You left before the service was over and you missed the best part." Pastor Walker continued

"Really? What was the best part?"

"Me preaching!"

"Oh…" I just stared at him. Joanna laughed. I looked at her then back at him…

"So that means you're going to have to come back again so you can hear me next time."

"Oh really?"

"Yea, what you think about that?"

"I think you need to time ya service and tell me exactly what time you go up. I'll come hear you preach then leave. But, I'm gon' tell you now… if you suck as bad as ya church do I'm walking out on you."

So I gave it another try. I went back to the church but I made Joanna go with me this time. On the way there she started questioning me.

"If he sucks are you really gone tell him?"

"Hell yea! Why not? What he gone do? Get mad?"

"He might…"

"Girl I don't give two farts… If you don't want me to say nothing don't ask me about it. I'm not gon' sit up here and lie to make nobody else feel good about themselves, what they're doing, or they foolishness. Those days are OVER!!!!"

We got there during the testimony service. Joanna looked at my face and knew I was annoyed. I was ready to go as soon as I walked in the building, but I encouraged myself to stay because I didn't want him to keep showing up at my house. I listened as one person after the next took the mic to talk about what God had done for them. Their tone of voice was so dry. It seemed like their speeches were forced or rehearsed. *If God just moved a mountain outta your way, brought you outta of the depths of hell, and blessed you... why do you sound dryer than a dessert in the summertime? You ain't got an ounce of excitement but you want me to be happy for you.* How does that work? As soon as they all were finished one by one they took off running, jumping, and yelling "Glory". The greatest part of it all was watching the weaves. Somebody really needed to tell those women to secure they hair before they went up in there acting a fool!

I couldn't help but stare as this one woman's ponytail. It was shouting harder than she was while she ran around the sanctuary crying screaming JESUS! The draw string was still tied around this small ball of hair, but the rest of the weave just flopped back and forth across the back of her head! As soon as the music stopped so did she. She immediately sat down and folded her arms as if nothing happened. One of the older women tapped her on her shoulder and handed her the dangling hair. She clipped it back in like it was never lost. As soon as everyone was quiet, Pastor Walker stood up and began preaching. I felt like he was talking directly to me but I didn't care. His topic was 'Looking Beyond the Mess and Hearing the Message'. No scriptural reference, he just started speaking. Though it sounded good I wasn't impressed. As soon as he opened the doors of the church I got up and walked out. Joanna quickly followed behind me. The entire ride home she laughed until tears poured from her eyes and snot shot from her nose.

First chance Pastor Walker got he was at my door. I saw him coming from the balcony so I walked outside. He joined me as I sat on the steps.

"What do you want?" I asked even though I knew.

"So what did you think about my message? Did it change your perception of the church? If it did change things did it change it enough for you to join? I think you'd be a great asset to the body of Christ."

"Do you want me to answer that honestly?"

"Always" he laughed.

"You really don't. My opinion gone hurt cha feelings."

"I'm a big boy. I can handle it… I swear."

 "First off You said to look past the mess to hear the message but what about the fact that the majority of the time the mess is coming from the messenger? How do you deal with the fact that the pastor is messier than the congregation? In my eyes, a mess is still a mess no matter how you dress it up. Or what about the fact that it's not enough real Christians to over shadow the church folks so for the people fresh off the streets looking for God church folks are the only representation of him they see. Why would I waste my time coming in the church when the streets are more honest? At least on the streets you know out the gate who can't be trusted but in the church, ya'll hide behind robes and titles.

Second, You talked about being an asset to the body of Christ but how can I be an asset to the body of Christ and I ain't got nothing to offer?

Third, I've paid quite a few visits to yo church back in the day, but I never stayed long enough to hear a complete sermon. I also looked a lot different then. You've only noticed me these last few times. I've been watching you so long that I can see right through you. You're shallow… You like a pretty face and little waist, but play it off like you're interested in the spirit. You use the scripture to your advantage to justify your wrong doings, just like everybody else. You have an excellent word game, and because of it, you know exactly which combo to put together to make it sound good. You give out just enough for people to be hooked on everything you say. I can mimic the relationship with God all day long. I've been in church for years… I can run and dance like the rest of them, but still leave and don't know Jesus or what a relationship with God is really about. I know all the church folks in there but have yet to see any for real for real Christians. I'm tired of faking and I'm tired of being around fake and phony people. I refuse to be another hypocritical Christian, corrupting somebody else. I'm coming into the doors of the church trying to get free, but instead I get bound by a new form of slavery. You just another fake ass Christian, using the word to his advantage."

"The church folk you talk about are for real Christians. They were all saved by grace".

"Naw… I went to a church once that actually had some for real Christians in it and they didn't act like the ones around here. It's a difference between being in church, playing church and the church being in you. For real Christians got a fire burning in them that causes them to want to minister to people right where they are with no shade or judgment. They are genuine! They can talk about God but can still be some earthly good. They do what the word says instead of just talking about it. For real Christians will be able to pray with you when you're going through instead of just telling you to 'pray about it'. It should be something different about you that people will want to know you because they can see the Jesus in you. The greatest accomplishment ya'll got going on in yo church is gaining a new title, but you ain't saved no souls. Why would I want to be in ya church? I see what ya'll really living like and all of us doing the same thing. Some of us even sleeping with the same people. I don't read my bible, but I see yo life and I don't see nothing different from mine. For some, your life is the only bible they'll ever read. So, what's so good about yo life that I wanna come worship with you? All ya'll look the same!

And why do ya'll collect 5 offerings? Tithes and Offering, Love Offering, Pastoral Offering, Peace Offering, and a damn building fund! Don't they pay you a salary? Why you got a offering too? On top of that… you been collecting for the same building fund for the last 10 years and ain't shit changed in yo building! You got a blown light in the bathroom and you still ain't got soap in there either! Ya'll filling the soap bottle with water! Ain't nothing in yo church from ya'll spirits to ya'll hands clean. Naw buddy… what I'm looking for ya'll ain't got it."

"You want people to give you a fair chance with no shade or judgment but you already got cha mind made up about all of us. Where is the justice at in that? The bible says judge not less ye be judged…"

"I'm not judging you. I'm telling you what I see. Personally, I can care less what any of you do. Like I said in the beginning… we ALL doing the same shit! With that being said… you can't save a dying soul in need, holding on to the same spirits we battling. You can't minister to me and you creeping with the same people I'm laying up with. You throwing out the same amount of liquor bottle and dropping the same amount of cuss words that I do you just do it behind closed doors, but you trying to save MY soul. It don't matter how many scriptures you quote on the loud speaker, me and you still gone die and go to the same hell. Every time I walk in the doors of your church I don't feel anything. Half the time, I'm fighting to keep my eyes open or I walk out feeling just like I did when I came in. Sometimes I feel worse depending on who I'm talking to."

"You don't feel nothing because you're not allowing God to use you. The anointing is falling and you just sit there like a bump on a log."

"Well then it should be so strong that it pimp slap the HELL outta me and make me jump to my feet! Fake don't move me."

"God don't force himself on nobody"

"Unlike Leadership!"

"Look if you don't want Him He gone let you be. I'm a military brat. When I got old enough I rebelled any which way I could think of. Then I found God, but I'm human too. I make mistakes. I fall down but the bible says a man falls seven times but will get back up again. I get back up, dust myself off, and keep going. I ain't no different than the rest of these jokers out here, but if you play with God long enough, eventually he gone snatch you up! You gone have to choose whose side you're on."

"Um… Well I choose to remain neutral and stay out the midst of the fake ass foolishness. I can do my sinning at home. I don't need to be in the multitude. I'm good."

"But you need to be covered and I can cover you. You also need the fellowship." He said this with a smile.

"Yea I bet you could but like I said… I'm good. I don't need you, fellowship, or people. I just need this bottle and a glass. The only decision I need to make is straight or with a chaser. So you have yourself a good day." I got up and walked to the house.

"Hey… you seem like you in a real hurt place."

"Yea but they say time heals all wounds so, we'll see."

I guess that triggered something in me because before I knew it tears tried to push their way out. I held my breath and swallowed them down, refusing to let them fall. When I walked in the door Joanna got on me.

"Damn! Did you have to be so ruthless?"

"Why not tell the truth? What the fuck I'm sparing feelings

for? Ain't nobody ever tried to spare mine?"

I popped some Tylenol so I wouldn't feel hung over the next day, grabbed the biggest glass I could find, filled it, and drank till I felt nothing. I drank until I couldn't even feel my heart beat and prayed that tomorrow never came.

Dear God,

Sometimes it's hard to even talk to you or find words for what I feel on the inside. I can say so many times that I'm sad or I'm hurt but that doesn't even begin to really speak on what I feel. Every day I wake up and take another breath feels like water is pouring down on my head, drowning me and I can't stop it. I keep seeking you because I need something to hold on to. Something to believe in, but I'm grasping for straws. I'm trying to believe in your miracles but all I see is misery. I breathe, swallow my tears and take the blows being delivered in stride. How do I let go? How do I get over it? I'm wrapped in this blanket of constant heaviness that's smothering me while I'm drowning. No matter how hard I push, press, and fight to break free I'm not winning. This journey of looking for love and trying to seek you seems like a losing battle. I heard that I'm supposed to look to you for my love and not people. The problem with that is, the ones that say this are all the ones that have somebody loving on them every day and lying next to them every night. Finding love in you is only half my problem. I don't feel you. I feel them. You see all and know all but yet my life has been one big struggle since as far back as I can remember. I came in this world fighting and I haven't stopped yet. I'm tired. I feel like the more I seek you the more hypocrites I encounter. In trying not to be one myself, I think I might be pulling further away from you.

Chapter 23

Every day I woke up I made it a point to drink more than I did the day before to keep from thinking, feeling, and to continue functioning like a normal person. Heading out to make another bottle run I ran into Jasmin who lived in the building next to mine. I knew who she was long before she ever knew I existed. She had an abundance of swag. Her sense of fashion was astonishing. I loved seeing her and her crew come in the door. Them parading in and out of their apartment was the highlight of most people's day. People would watch their apartment door waiting to see what creative fashion they were going to walk out with.

Hanging out with them was like an elevation into an elite social setting that everybody desired to be in. Only the cream of the crop made it in. Though they were a very private bunch they were admired by many. I watched them from afar for quite some time before I finally mustered up enough courage to speak. I ran into them at a local Target and decided to finally say something.

"Hello Reverend Jas, Reverend Kyle, Chelsea, Jacob, Calvin, and Kaleb". If looks could kill, I would've dropped dead immediately! The death stares pierced me with no response.

"Who the hell are you? And how do you know my name?" Jasmin snapped.

"We live in the same apartment complex. I'm in the building next door to you and I've been visiting your church for the past several months."

"Oh, sorry… Hi."

I laughed then continued on my way. From that moment on anytime we'd see each other I'd laugh. Their reactions amused me. A couple weeks later all the laughing and teasing turned into a conversation. We talked about any and everything. Those conversations developed into a friendship. It seemed like every day our friendship grew stronger and stronger. Reverend Jas helped me to slow down on my drinking. In them, I was going to find the love that had been long sought after, but never fully discovered. In them I thought I had found some of the things I had been yearning for. I adored the love and affection they showed to one another. Before I knew it, they began treating me just like they treated each other. While doing so they taught me how to be affectionate, they taught me the difference between gentle touches and those I was accustom to. I learned to love the idea of being loved all over again.

At some point my lines blurred between infatuation and love because when Jasmin told me her and her husband Kyle were in love with me and wanted to be more than just friends I fell for it. I thought love had written itself a brand-new chapter and for once had included me in it. When we first started out I was wined, dined, and romanced in ways that never existed for me before. It's often said that you can't help who you fall in love with, but during times like these it really made me wonder… I never in a million years thought anyone could hold my entire heart in the palm of their hands. But, it happened. They had my heart in a state of limbo and I stood there, watching it beat. I thought I really knew what love was with them. I thought in them lay everything I had ever wanted. I thought I'd hit an all-time high. Especially when he proposed a few months after we all started exclusively seeing each other.

It was a magical moment for me. I was sitting in the living room in the recliner watching television when he walked in the room. Jasmin followed close behind him.

Suddenly, he got down on one knee, took my hand and asked me to marry him. Jasmin stood off to the side, grinning from ear to ear. When I said yes, he placed the ring on my hand. It was a beautiful blue topaz white gold diamond ring. It was gorgeous! We spent the rest of the night simply outlining what this new arrangement consisted of. My only restriction was that I couldn't sleep with anyone else besides them, which I was ok with. We prayed together, studied the word together, and fellowshipped with other Christians who had relationships like ours. I prided myself on being a great wife! I did whatever was needed and required of me.

When Kyle lost his job, I was right there to pick up the pieces and help carry the torch to keep the family running smoothly. I worked multiple jobs to make sure everybody's needs were met because I felt like it was my duty. For the first three years everything seemed great. My heart wanted to believe they truly loved me even though my mind told me a different story. My mind was telling me that I didn't belong with them! That no matter how long I stayed with the pack… I mean the family… and stayed in my made up lane, they'd turn on me. But, I didn't listen. I ignored my better judgment and continued to play my role. I was an outcast trying to convince myself I was a part of the crew.

Every day was another lesson learned that could never be forgotten. There was always something about me I needed to change or improve on, according to them. Words dug wounds in me the size of craters. Their actions along with others aided the words in drilling deeper, yet I was too emotional… I was too sensitive… I wasn't strong enough… When I would take a deep breath, and swallow my tears I was told I wasn't a man… I needed to talk and release those feelings. On the flip side of things, I was too intense, too needy, too clingy, too demanding, too controlling... I just wanted to be loved. Yet, love turned into a laundry list of requirements and restrictions I needed to meet in order to get it. Most of which were difficult to live up to, but I tried.

I always had to prove myself. I needed to be perfect for imperfect people to keep their love and they capitalized on it. I was a shape-shifting chameleon so I never stopped transforming into who or what they wanted me to be. No matter what I did, it was NEVER enough. I had to prove I was trustworthy, I had to prove my love, I had to prove my loyalty. Everything was a privilege, including sex. Sex was a privilege I could only have when I was ALLOWED to get it. Sex, like most things in our relationship, was one-sided. Too desperate to allow myself to believe that this wasn't real, I gave away the remaining pieces of me that couldn't be taken. In them, I lost what little of Karen I had left. I was their best kept secret. Very few people knew about this relationship between the three of us. So badly I wanted to believe in love and family. I tried to use them to fill voids in me that had been there for years, but they couldn't. The voids of missing my mama, loneliness, needing love, emptiness, abandonment, and a whole lot more. The list could go on and on.

They just managed to do something others couldn't. They destroyed me internally. I had blinders on that caused me to not be able to see things in reality. In years three through seven, those blinders began to lift more and more each year. I was the side chick playing a leading role but didn't see it. I would be the one left out in the end. I thought we were equal when in actuality I was a third-class citizen allowed to hang around. Maybe it was the guilt of our love for each other that began consuming us as we strived to be proper Christians. Maybe it was me seeing them for who they really were. Either way, my heart hurt in ways I never thought it could. I thought I had been through it all but nothing I'd ever gone through could prepare me for what I was about to endure emotionally.

On every public trip, I walked behind them as they

cuddled and held hands. I enviously watched them, waiting to be noticed. I was invisible in public, but behind closed doors we were making love (just having sex) nightly, trying to build a family. I convinced myself that I could feel the love they had for me in each stroke as they fucked me every which way but wrong. Having sex wasn't easy because of my history with it but through them, I learned to accept it as something natural. I actually started to really like it sometimes. During the times where my nerves would begin to get the best of me as he switched positions, she'd rest her hand on my shoulder.

"it's alright baby. Relax and enjoy it". I didn't always know how but I was conditioned to go along with whatever.

"Stop holding your breath… breathe and enjoy." She was my lover and my coach.

I was often silent during the act itself, which caused him to wonder if he was any good. As many times as I'd had sex before, I never learned to say anything or respond to anyone to reassure them they were doing a great job. The majority of the time I just laid there waiting for them to finish. I treated him the same way until she taught me.

"If you like it, say something. Moan, scream, talk, something…" I clung to her words like a newborn clinging to its mother's breast for nourishment.

Then I began to do it. I imitated sounds I'd heard from others until they became real sounds of enjoyment to me. I was hanging on to a dream that I was frantically striving to make my reality. I was in love with the idea of having someone who could give me the love that life never did. A love that had brought me just as much comfort as food. Because I didn't have someone to love me like I needed, food became my "go to". It became my passion… my joy.

Together, the two of us had an unexplainable love

affair. It had a way of soothing my unreachable damaged places and holding them. With each bite, I swallowed one emotion after another. At two and three in the morning I'd cook whole meals. I'd sit down and eat every last bit of it then lie back down and go to sleep. I'd go to the grocery store and clear out the baking isle to go back home and bake. I'm talking whole cake, trays of cupcakes, and sheets of cookies that would be gone in a matter of days. I ate until I felt better then I'd go back to sleep. It wasn't until I was sitting on the couch, finishing off a gallon of ice cream and listening to myself breathing that I really began to look at myself. There was a slight snore with each breath as if I was sleeping, but I was wide awake. Walking was a chore for me. I felt drained and out of breath just walking from the living room to the bathroom in an 875 sq ft. apartment.

As I ate my emotions, my body was spreading. I went from a size 12 to a 26 and I was quickly knocking at the door of 300 pounds. I didn't want to let it go though. Food was my miseries best friend and the two desperately needed each other. The more weight I gained the less Jasmin wanted to come by my house to hang out. She said it was because I lived on the 2nd floor and she didn't feel like pulling the stairs. However, I noticed that she faithfully went to chill at our friend Cassandra's house, who also stayed on the 2nd floor. She lived in another building around the corner from us. Cassandra, a.k.a "Sandy", was a friend of mine that I met a few years back, when I was apartment hunting. We clicked. I introduced the two of them and the three of us had hung out regularly ever since.

Unfortunately, Sandy was often caught in the middle of the silent war Jasmin and I had going on. She didn't really know the truth of our relationship. She'd often get upset at the way Jasmin disrespected me but got tired of addressing it. She constantly said something to me about it but I'd always tell her to just leave it alone. Half the time, I honestly didn't even hear the stuff Jasmin said because I was so accustomed to tuning her out. I didn't really start to pay attention to what she said until one Saturday night when the two of us were hanging out she jumped up and said

"Alright I'm about to go. I have to go pick Kyle up from work." Jasmin announces.

I was somewhat confused by the statement because she never announced it before. I felt like it was a sweet sendoff, but I ignored it. I waivered while trying to decide if I was going to ride with her like I normally did. She continued to make vague statements about the ride. I conveniently ignored them, as I do much of what she says now. I go to get in the car but she stops me.

"Where are you going?" She asks.

"I'm going to ride with you to get Kyle."

"Oh, you can't go this time."

"Why not?"

"Because you've put on a lot of extra weight and I don't want the transmission to go out."

With hidden hurt feelings, I stared at her. I couldn't believe she actually had the nerve to say that, seeing as how I didn't put the weight on alone. She was eating right alongside me most of the time. She was bigger than I was and always had been.

"So you saying I'm too fat to ride in your car now?"

"No. It's just that we are already having problems with the car and I'm trying not to drive it that much. I don't want all our weights put together to kill the transmission. That's all…"

"Uh huh… Yea that's what it is."

So I went to go hang out with Cassandra instead. When I

got to her house she asked "Where's Jasmin?"

"She went to pick up Kyle from work."

"Oh, why didn't you go? You always ride with her…"

"Because I'm too fat to ride now. I'm gone mess up the transmission in her car." She looked at me with the same look on her face that I had on mine. You could tell she was pissed and I laughed.

"Stop looking like that! This shit has gotten so ridiculous that you just have to laugh at it…" I chuckled.

"Man Kay… stop lying on that girl. She ain't told you that bullshit!"

"Umph… Yes, the hell she did! As a matter a fact, the conversation went like this… and I quote word for word…

'Where are you going?

'I'm going to ride with you to get Kyle'

'Oh, you can't go this time'

'Why not?'

'Because you've put on a lot of extra weight and I don't want the transmission to go out.'

 "I proceeded to say to her…" 'So, you saying, I'm too fat to ride in your car now?' "and she said"

'No. It's just that we are already having problems with the car and I'm trying not to drive it that much. I don't want all our weights put together to kill the transmission. That's all.'

"YEA FUCKING RIGHT!!!!!" Cassandra yelled. "If that was the case then she would've said that bullshit to begin with. She was just trying to clean it up because you asked her was she trying to say you were too fat to ride in her car. So the answer to yo question is HELL YEA! She saying you too fat to ride in her car. Has she looked in the mirror lately?

That BITCH bigger than you! What the Fuck she mean?"

"Just let it go friend. It doesn't matter..." I tried to get Cassandra to calm down.

"Yes the fuck it does matter and that's yo problem! You too damn nice and you let too much shit go. Stop fucking taking everything that muthafucker dishes out to you, acting like it's ok! You half ass open up yo mouth and say shit and act like it doesn't faze you when it clearly does. Because you eat everything under the sun every time yo feelings get hurt and if you ain't gone say nothing I am. That shit was out of fucking order!"

"Just let it go. It's ok..."

"Nope... because I don't like how she treating my friend."

She picks up the phone and calls Jasmin. "Hello Jas..." She puts her phone on speaker phone.

"Hey girl what's up?" Jasmin answers.

"How the fuck you gone tell Kay she too fat to ride in yo car? What kind of shit is that to say to somebody and you bigger than she is? You have the nerve to call her yo best friend? That ain't the way you treat your fucking best friend! You treat her like she some random ass stranger trying to be your biggest fan!"

"NOOOOO! I swear I didn't mean it like that and I wish she would stop saying that! I was just saying that because we were already having car issues and I didn't want to add her weight to it and risk messing up the car completely. I really didn't mean it how it sounded. I tried to explain it to her."

"Naw... you meant it how you said it because if that was the case, you would've said it differently the first time. Not start trying to clean it up once people start responding to it. And as much as that damn girl done, done for you... you wrong as fuck for treating her the way you do! I told her she need to stop being your friend."

"I'm sorry I..." Sandy hung up the phone before Jasmin could continue.

Then she began dialing another number. I hear a male talking in the background and I'm wondering what she's doing. I just sat watching her.

"Hello, thank you for calling Johnson Automotive. How may I help you?"

"Yes... may I speak with a mechanic please?" Sandy requested.

"Yes, I'm a mechanic. How may I help you?"

"Can you answer a question for me? If a person weighs about 280 pounds can they mess up the transmission on a car? And YES... this is a real question."

"Well no... I'm going to say they can't, but without looking at how bad a shape the car is in I can't really say for sure. Is the car drivable?"

"Yes it is. It drives from Carmel to Westfield, Lawrence and Lebanon almost every day."

"You do realize those cities are about an hour away?" The mechanic asks.

"Yes sir I do. But my friend weighs about 280 pounds, maybe a little more. And someone told her she couldn't ride in their car because her weight was gone mess up they transmission!"

"They were just being mean to your friend..."

"Ok, thank you! That's all I needed to know."

"You have a good night ma'am."

"You too."

We look at each other and I change the subject.

Chapter 24

The next day, Sandy and I were hanging out chilling when Jasmin called. She asked me to trail her to the car shop so they could work on her car. Then she wanted me to bring her back home. Sandy responded before I could.

 "Hell Naw you can't! Tell her she too fat to fit in yo fucking car!" Those words were followed by a deep eye roll. I laughed and told Jasmin I'd be over in a few minutes.

"Why the fuck are you going?"

"Because I want to ask the mechanic if my weight can affect the transmission."

"I already got an answer to that for you."

"I know, but I want to do it in front of her…"

"I guess… Let me know what happens."

"Ok I will."

I left to meet Jasmine and trail her. When we arrived at the first auto repair place, I waited till she finished talking to the mechanic. She was getting an exam and estimate done on her car and I spoke out.

"Excuse me sir…" He turns to look at me, so I continue.

"Just out of curiosity… can my weight kill the transmission if I got in that car?" He laughed hysterically.

"Hell naw! You will need something a whole lot bigger than you to kill the transmission."

"Ok, thank you!" He walked back in the shop still laughing.

She didn't like the estimate so we went to the next repair shop to get a quote. I asked that mechanic the same thing and got the same response.

"Where did you get that from?" He asked as he laughed.

"Oh, she told me I was too fat to get in her car and she didn't want my weight to kill her transmission." He looked at her then looked at me.

"And you still letting her get in YOUR car? You a good one..." He mugged Jasmin and shook his head.

"I really wish you wouldn't say that. I'm sorry. I didn't mean it like that."

"Say what? What you say?" I just looked at her, walked to my car and got in.

I dropped Jasmin off at her house and was heading to meet up with Sandy. By now she had gotten really good at reading in between the lines so, I planned to tell her the truth about everything. When Sandy suggested we go out to eat I thought that would be the perfect time to fill her in, but I declined the offer. I was recently laid off both my jobs and I had to wait two weeks before I received my last checks. Those would be just enough to cover the rent and it would be four to six weeks before unemployment kicked in. I was already living paycheck to pay check and had started having a lot of health issues, which was making it increasingly difficult to stay afloat. There was no money left in between pay periods once the bills were paid and the prescriptions were refilled.

I had been really sick for months and in excruciating pain. The doctors had no idea what was causing it so I was basically a guinea pig. They tested different theories trying to figure out what was going on. On top of that, I started having difficulty breathing. I had an upper respiratory infection, asthma, and bronchitis to add to the list of issues going on. I was taking 11 different medications just to get through the day. I didn't have any money to buy food let alone go out to eat, but Sandy refused to accept no for an answer. Jasmin had also resurfaced and asked where we were going. At that point, Sandy thought it would be rude not to invite her to dinner with us. Before Jasmin got into the car Sandy reassured me.

"Hey… I know you don't want to go because you don't have any money. Well, don't worry about it, I got you covered. I really want you to go. Plus, you need to get out the house anyway."

I was hesitant but I accepted the invite. She was right. I did need to get out the house. Since I had been unemployed, when I wasn't on a job interview or feeling out a job application, I was just sitting in the house or laying in a hospital bed. I had been going through a lot so hanging out with friends was long overdue.

At dinner, Jasmin was on a roll, as usual with the rude and out of line comments. I got up and went to the bathroom. When I left the table, the lady sitting across from us excused herself to go to the bathroom as well. On my way there the waitress stopped me.

"Excuse me… but is that other lady at the table your friend?" She asked.

"Yes… we are all best friends…"

The lady from the other table looked puzzled. "You know… I excused myself because I wanted to know the same thing."

The waitress continued "I heard the things she was saying to you and you didn't say anything."

"When a person is showing their true colors, sometimes it's not even worth commenting" I said. "Anyway, I've gotten so used to ignoring her that I honestly didn't hear half the stuff she was saying."

"Well, you should definitely start paying attention because with friends like her I'd hate to see what your enemies look like." The waitress walked off and I continued to head for the restroom.

"Baby, you need to be careful who you call friend" the lady from the other table warned. "That ain't nowhere near a friend at all."

I looked at the lady as we walked into the bathroom. Once we finished and walked back to the table, she watched us the rest of the evening. As I sat down, the waitress came back to the table.

"The other ladies have ordered. Would you like to order something?"

"No, I'm good. Thank you."

Jasmin looked at me and whispered, "You don't have any money, do you?"

I shook my head no to see if she was going to offer to feed me. Instead, she turned to Sandy.

"Tonight, is going to be my treat. I'm going to pay for your food."

"I don't need nobody to pay for my food. I got me!" Sandy replied.

"You know Karen ain't got no money to eat but instead of you buying her meal, you wanna buy mine?" Sandy rolled her eyes and shook her head.

"Kay I got you. Order you whatever you want to eat."

"And if she don't I do. So, if you don't have enough for her and you need more money, let me know. I got her." The lady at the table across from us chimed in. "And I don't care what you say… that ain't yo DAMN friend! And you need to get rid of her ass!"

Wow! I couldn't believe it. My so called best friend and lover wasn't willing to feed me but a perfect stranger was… I felt ashamed and too embarrassed to eat anything. I hated with a passion that I didn't have any money. I felt low and poor. There were many illegal things I could have done to make ends meet. I didn't because I called myself trying to live right, but every day that was becoming more and more difficult. I went from working two jobs to none and unemployment was taking too long to kick in.

 "I got her covered, but thank you…" Sandy said.

"No, that's ok. I'm good." I hung my head in shame of my situation.

"Don't sit there sad and hungry…"

"It's ok. I'm used to this…"

"Fuck that! It ain't never ok to be hungry as long as you're my friend! And if I can help it you won't be either." She flagged the waitress over.

"Yes ma'am…"

"I'd like to place a to go order. Can I have an order of the Chicken Cajun Pasta dish and an extra bag of garlic bread sticks?"

"Yes, ma'am. I'll get that order prepared for you right away."

"Thank you" I said sadly. We sat the rest of the time in silence. When the bill came Jasmin paid her bill and walked away from the table. I got up next.

"Naw don't go out there yet. Wait for me cause I don't want her saying shit else to you!" Sandy paid for us and we went to the car. She dropped Jasmin off at home and told me not to get out the car.

"Do you have food upstairs?" She asked.

"No" I shamefully responded. She backed out and we drove to the grocery store.

"Get as much stuff as you want."

I did as Sandy said. I got as many meals as I could that would stretch out over time so that I wouldn't have to worry about being hungry for a while. Every two weeks Sandy took me to the store to get food whether I had some left over or not. She also periodically came over to check my kitchen to see how much food I had. If she felt like it was low she'd go buy groceries and drop it off to me.

Chapter 25

After the restaurant incident Jasmin and I couldn't last 15 minutes in a room with each other without arguing so the three of us stopped hanging out altogether. It bothered me that no matter the subject, Jasmin had to be right about everything. Her philosophy was that she was never wrong and even when she was wrong she wasn't gonna admit it, so she was still right. That bothered me most of all, which led us to argue all the time. I always wanted to explain why I was right and she always wanted to explain why everything going wrong was my fault. Those arguments led into many other arguments about everything else. Normally, I would accept the blame. I would justify their actions and behaviors, rationalize it to myself, and make excuses for how they treated me. But, I got sick of it.

I began to voice my true feelings about the things I had apparently ignored for years and protested the consistently, bias and unfair treatment. I started to acknowledge their pettiness and I no longer bit my tongue for either of them. I couldn't tolerate the times where she and I would be upset with one another and would be ignoring each other. He would stop talking to me because she would stop talking to me, until he wanted to have sex. Then he'd act like nothing ever happened. She would keep score of every time I did something she considered wrong, then throw it in my face as soon as I called her out on something she was doing to me that I didn't like. He never let my past be my past.

He always brought it up to justify why I just couldn't go with the grain on things. Even if I had gotten over something, he'd still throw it up to prove his point. A lot of the time, it felt like they were re-digging old wounds instead of focusing on the issue at hand. If one got pissed off about something, they both were pissed off about it. More often than not, I would have to play the guessing game to figure out what I did wrong this time. Our happy little arrangement was far from happy and though we had our good days, when it was bad it was really bad.

I'd gone through dozens of experiences before and the price I paid for all of them was always more expensive than the obstacle itself. The cost was already great but this time it was more than even I could bear. She hurt me in places and with depths that I never thought I could be hurt. She didn't fight fair. They were petty so when I fought one I fought them both. They would unite as one and I was left alone to fend for myself until the dust settled. It was in those moments that I began to see more and more of who they really were. Yes, I got hurt physically but those wounds tend to heal. It was the emotional devastations that crippled me constantly, but they were like my kryptonite. She made me feel important, beautiful, wanted but then in the same breath I wasn't enough.

I hung in there until the bitter end. More and more each day I had a threesome with brokenness, hurt, and anger. I made love to them constantly. Every blow, every lying whisper of I love you... I need you... I want you... Every push, every shove...I took. Each time I was grabbed by my neck and left dangling in the air while the lights faded... I took. I'd hide my tears refusing to let them fall. Crying was for babies and I was a grown ass woman. Too grown to cry over hurt feelings.

She was in my head and she knew it. She also knew I'd do anything for the sake of love and I hung in there because I loved them both. Every once in a blue moon when he would get sick of hearing Jasmin and I argue, he would try to be the peace maker between the two of us. It didn't last long because as soon as she would redirect her wrath towards him he would instantly choose her side again. Then the relationship became one sided again because it was her side he chose. Then there was a different type of battle that occurred because they were both strategic. I just reacted out of emotion because I was never enough. We had both been through a lot of shit in our lives. I thought that would keep us closer together since it was the bond that connected us in the first place. It turned out to be the complete opposite instead.

I worked and attempted to save so I could start my life over somewhere else…yet again. I wanted to find the happiness I continuously heard people talk about but only seen in glimpses for a moment here and there. I was done. We were done. But… I got surprised with pretty dresses, shoes and jewelry at random. Along with that came a beautiful card and an abundance of 'I'm sorry… I didn't mean it'. I allowed myself to get suckered back in with the artificial sincerity and tears being served up. I was right back in the cycle. This went on for yet another year until it came to a head again on a warm night in September.

The day had been rough. Everything that could go wrong did. I felt so lonely and needed some company bad, but I didn't feel like calling anyone. There came a knock on my door. It was Jasmin and Kyle with pizza and vodka. It was time for a much needed turn up. As the night progressed we continued to eat, laugh, and talk. It wasn't long before the sex games started and together, the three of us, began to make love to one another. This was something we had done so many times before. As our bodies entangled with one another, Kyle disappeared and Jasmin and I played alone. My tongue flicked her clitoris until it started to swell. As she moaned loudly he reappeared in the doorway with another drink. He finished his cup and rejoined the party. He flipped me to my back and slid in. As he entered I told myself this was love. It was the love that I had been needing, wanting, and searching for. Nothing or no one could take it away from me. A few strokes in he stops.

"I'm going to vomit!" He reports.

"Get yo ass up and go to the bathroom!" We both yell, but he doesn't move.

"Go to the bathroom!" I say it again but still nothing.

Instead he lays there until it comes. Pizza and liquor all over my sheets and my floor. I jump out of the way before it lands on me. I'm sick to my stomach. I can't believe this shit! This seriously did not just happen! When he finished, they began arguing as I stripped my bed and put my clothes on. I didn't have a washer or dryer and at 1 am I was not going to drag these sheets to my car to look for a laundry service. As I stood there in disbelief, I watched as he semi cleaned the floor. Jasmin kept apologizing. He, on the other hand, wasn't sorry at all.

"You ain't got to apologize for me to this bitch!"

"Bitch… oh I'm a bitch now? Naw you the bitch! I just take note and learn from the best!"

"Man fuck you! You ain't shit but a hoe and that's all you'll ever be!" He staggers into the hall. We started arguing but he suddenly grabbed my head and pushed it into the wall. I was stunned because he had never put his hands on me before. "You ain't shit but a hoe!"

"I'm a hoe but you was just fucking me though."

"Yes you a hoe! You always been a hoe and hell I'm human. I ain't gone turn down no free pussy! If you giving it, I'm gone take it."

My love for him was no different than my love for her. I was heartbroken. She pulled him out the door, but I could still hear them arguing in the parking lot. I followed them home to make sure she was ok. The arguing continued. Eventually she put me out. The next day he called me to come over and apologize for disrespecting me. In my head, a drunken mind speaks sober thoughts and that night I found out what he truly thought of me. He was just putting on a show all these years to get what he wanted out of me. The last seven years of my life was a lie and I told them both as much and left. The world that I had built up in my head with the last ounce of love that remained, was just shattered in front of me. I was at a loss. Too hurt to breathe deeply and too empty to form words to speak.

Hold it in Karen… Don't lose it. Keep your cool, I told myself. Breathe baby… breathe. Hang in there. Everything is going to be ok. I could hear these thoughts running through my head, but I was too dumbfounded to react. I needed air. I needed to clear my head. I headed for my car. When I went to get in my car it sounded funny so, I took it a couple miles up the road to get it looked at. It was going to be a couple hours before I could pick it up. When I went back to the house he continued to try to talk to me. I listened to what he had to say. Again, everything in me told me to leave and be done with them. But, as always, I didn't take heed. My need to be loved had me blind to reality. After all, the things I subjected myself to were a lot better than the things I had been through. However, it was time for me to stop hurting myself.

I let a few days pass and I decided that was it. I had made up in my mind that I was leaving and today would be the day that I told Jasmin it was over. I had rehearsed it and wavered on it several times. The truth was that I really wanted to be loved by someone but the drama was just entirely too much. We had been fussing so much that we both made an agreement that today would be the day we'd get along, by any means necessary. I allowed myself to be convinced, yet again, that this was where my love resided. This time, it was both of them together surprising me with pretty shoes, dresses, shawls and jewelry. Taking me shopping in places like Neiman Marcus and Bloomingdales, stores that I would've never stepped foot in had it not been for them. I was floored by the treatment I was getting, along with more beautiful cards and more apologies. I fell for it again! I must be out of my damn mind!

Chapter 26

Everything appeared to be just like it was 6 years ago when we first got involved with one another. We sat in the living room and talked while watching tv. After a while, she came to me and began kissing me passionately. She gently took my hand and guided me to the bedroom. I stood just inside the doorway and watched her. She moved around the room clearing off the bed and then came back to me. She began kissing me again. I let her. Out of nowhere she grabbed me by my throat. I felt myself in the air and then flying. BAM!... a loud bump... Thud... another one... Stinging pains ripped through me.

I blinked quickly to try to regain my focus, but all I could see was bright lights. The kind you get when you've been staring directly into the sun. I moved around trying to get up, even though I couldn't focus. My head was throbbing. I had been thrown into the wall. I slid down only to bounce off the head board. As she grabbed my legs she snatched me down, causing me to hit the head board a second time. I wasn't completely off it yet in the first place. As she yanked me towards her she was stripping me out of my clothes.

It felt like one swoop and I was naked from the waist down. I tried to slide back onto the bed but I was still disoriented. Pains shot all through my body. My head and back ached. She grabbed my legs and pulled me towards her. There was a sharp stabbing between my legs. It continued non-stop. Still trying to register what was happening, I tried to focus to figure out what the hell she had in her hand. Why was this happening? I once again stopped struggling and simply laid there. I've been in this position before. I began to talk to myself as tears rolled down my face.

"Shhh… don't cry. It's ok. Just hang in there. It'll all be over soon." I repeated it over and over again till it was over. I curled up in a ball in shock at what had just happened. She lay next to me.

"Damn… I think I just raped you… Go wash yo ass."

"You did…"

I slid off the bed and attempted to stand. My legs were shaking and throbbing. I hurt so bad. I picked my clothes up off the floor and held on to the wall till I got to the bathroom. I rinsed, dressed and left…. never speaking of it again. It was days before the physical pain went away and I buried the emotional scars with the rest of them. I should've left then but I stayed. No matter how bad things got, I could still see the good in them. I stayed because of all the things they did right instead of leaving for everything that was done wrong. Despite anything my mind told me, my heart needed to believe the love was real. In their love lied the last ounce of hope I had to hold on to and I needed it bad. I needed to believe.

Dear God,

I'm in a real, real dark place right now. Hurt doesn't even begin to describe what I'm feeling. I feel so low and disgusting. I feel like I'm losing my mind and I'm doing everything I can to stay sane. I need somebody to love me. I know I'm supposed to look to you for my love… that you'll supply all my needs but that's easier said than done. I'm trying everything I can to hold on to you… I'm trying to believe in you but all I keep seeing is bad and all I keep feeling is more and more devastation. I've asked you to be with me, to hold me, to love me but at night I'm still laying in the bed lonely. I'm crying myself to sleep and looking for what I need in other people who are supposed to be your followers. They killing me internally. How much more do you think I can hold... I WANT TO DIE... I WISH I WAS DEAD... WHY ARE YOU KEEPING ME HERE TO SUFFER? WHY WON'T YOU JUST LET ME DIE? I HAVE NO DESIRE TO LIVE OR DO ANYTHING ELSE... GOD!!!! I'm standing here with my arms stretched up. I'm reaching into thin air, trying to find something to hold on to but there's nothing there. You said if I made the first step you'd meet me where I was. Well I've made several attempts and you're nowhere to be found. Nobody loves me. Not even you, but I'm supposed to be ok in all this. How? Something's gotta give. I can't keep going on like this.... I'm dying inside and going through hell outside. I just want somebody... anybody... to love me, want me, hold me, give me a reason to smile. My days go from dark to darker every day. Where is the light at the end of the tunnel? Where is the sunshine? I feel like I'm talking to myself because I never get an answer from you. I keep talking to you because you got my mama but I'm beginning to wonder if she's just gone forever because this God that everybody keep talking about doesn't exist. The one I see is just as bad as they are. Maybe everybody's lying! I can't live and I can't die. Life keeps torturing me and death keeps rejecting me. WHAT THE FUCK!

I no longer had the energy to pretend to be happy or content with this relationship. I can't breathe in it, it hurts. Every breath I take I can feel the heaviness of my heart.

"I'm done. I can't do this no more… I'm out" I took my ring off.

"You're not leaving!"

"This is not going to be an argument or debate. I'm done" I sat the ring on the counter.

"So you really doin' this? You got somebody else? Bitch you really gon' let the next muthafucka break up our family! Every family has its problems. You gon' throw 6 years away like I it ain't mean shit! Who you fucking? You gon' break up our family to go be with somebody else?"

"So what if I fucked somebody else... since you don't want to fuck me!" Suddenly, I started seeing flashes of light. I kept blinking my eyes to try to regain my focus but now my head was hurting.

"And there's plenty more where that came from. You want to run that shit by me again?" She dared me.

I looked at the wall "this bitch just hit me..."

I picked up the small wooden cutting board from the table and threw it with everything I had in me. It flew towards her face, barely missing. The breeze from the speed of the board danced across the side of her face as it flies by, hits the wall and splits into pieces. As we argued, the rage of our tempers grew more and more. The higher our tempers flared, the more objects hurled back and forth. From one room to another we went, with nothing standing in our way but space. If I didn't already have a strong bob and weave game, I was gone get one today. Bottles, shoes, dishes, vases, lamps... If I could grab a hold of it, I threw it. I guess she got tired of throwing objects because before I knew it she was in a rage. She charged at me with a knife faster than I could react to it. *"Damn! I can't believe this bitch just cut me!"* I said to myself, in shock, as I looked down to see the blood rushing through my shirt. Pains blazing higher than our tempers tore through me. My knees become weak. I grabbed the arm of the couch. When she saw my hand covered in blood she snapped out of her rage, dropped the knife, grabbed some towels, and ran to me placing them over the wound.

"Baby I'm so sorry. I was angry. I didn't mean it. You just

pissed me off!"

"Get the fuck off me… Don't touch me… MOVE"! Tears uncontrollably roll down my face as I take deep breaths, attempting to suck them up. I push her away from me.

"Hell, I said I was sorry… damn! Move yo hand and let me fucking help you!"

"Naw, FUCK you! Get the FUCK off me!" I push her away again. The tears finally stop.

She throws my arm out the way yelling "Dammit! I said I'm fucking sorry! I didn't mean it!"

Teeth clamped tightly refusing to let another tear fall I said "Yea you meant the shit! Because if you didn't you wouldn't have done it. SO GET THE FUCK AWAY FROM ME! I'LL HELP MY DAMN SELF!!!" I scream.

I get up heading to the bathroom my legs felt like limp noodles. My side felt like it was ripping apart with each step I took. As I stand in the mirror looking at the tears in my shirt I lift it slowly to see how much damage has been done to me this time. She slit my skin from my belly button to my back. I took my towel ran it under warm water and continuously wiped the blood. The more I wiped the more enraged I became.

I became infuriated by the sight of my own blood dripping from my body. It ran down my leg, soaked the towel, onto the floor…Literally the only thing I saw was red. I began screaming at myself in the mirror, threw the toothbrush holder at my reflection and shattered the entire glass! Then I turned my focus to her. The real source of my anger in that moment. I ran up the hall toward her yelling.

"I hate myself and it's because of you! You are such a bitch and the problem with you is that you don't even know it! You don't love me. You never did!"

As I charged toward her I picked up a lamp and threw it! I

was aiming straight for her nose. I imagined it was the bullseye on a dart board! She screamed and ducked. The lamp hit the wall behind her. The porcelain bottom splintered into piece and the shade landed on her head.

"You treated me like shit and I let you. Yea I'm stupid but BITCH you're dead! Or at least you gon' be because I'm gon' kill yo ass today!"

She jumped to her feet and ran toward the kitchen. I knew I had to get to her before she got that knife again. So, I lunged at her and tackled her back to the floor. She was bigger than me so I knew I wouldn't be on top for long but while I was up there I had to make an impact.

"First you rape me then you stab me! You can't say enough sorry's! Bloomingdale's and Macy's ain't gon' save yo ass this time. If you loved me you should have let me go cuz now you gotta die. And don't worry…I'm not go leave yo kids without a momma like I was left without mine. I'm gon' send them to wherever you goin. Oh yea…and yo husband'll be right behind them. I loved you and yo whole family and all ya'll did was shit on me! So, I have no sympathy or mercy for any of ya'll. I hope you really know Jesus like you say you do because you about to meet him face-to-face."

I picked up a piece of the broken glass that spewed out from the bathroom into the hall and began slicing her face and throat. She grabbed my waist digging her hand into my open wound while hitting me with the other hand attempting to get me off of her. I continued slicing away at her. The neighbor downstairs called the police because of all the loud bumping and screaming going on.

We heard the knocking at the door but was too busy fighting to respond. The door was still unlocked from when I came in earlier so the police let themselves in and pulled us apart. As one of the officers grabbed me away from her I continued kicking, screaming, and trying to get back at her.

"Calm down" he yelled.

"Fuck you! I'm gon' kill this bitch and everybody else too!"

"If you don't settle down…"

"Fuck you! Fuck you! Get the fuck off me!"

"Get her outta here take her ass to jail" Jasmin yelled.

"It's ok. As soon as I get out I'ma wait till everybody in this bitch go to sleep and kill all you muthafuckas watch!" I yell as I cracked the slyest most evil smile I could. If I was looking in the mirror I would guess it looked like a cross between chuckie and mommy dearest".

The officers handcuffed me and escorted me out the house as I sat in the back of the squad car the bottled up tears began to pour out. As the car began to drive away all I could do was cry. The more my emotions exploded the louder my cry became. My pain erupted into sobbing screams of anguish.

"These bitches done raped me, beat me, cut me, and tortured me all in the name of Jesus but I'm the one goin' to jail. LET ME DIE GOD LET ME DIE!!! WHY WON'T YOU JUST LET ME DIE?" I screamed out.

Two police officers radio in. "We have a 27 yo AA female who just tore up the inside of an apartment and threatened to kill everyone in it! We have her in the cage right now in handcuffs and I think we gone need a strait jacket!"

"That wasn't no fuckin threat it was a promise! Where the fuck y'all taking me? When I get out of here ima fuck all y'all up! Ain't nobody listening to me. You don't even hear what the fuck I'm saying cause don't nobody give a fuck!

We pull up at this big white building that looks like a college campus. We walk through these tented doors. There a woman awaits with 2 big Debo looking men.

"Hello, Karen I'm Dr. Black"

"How the fuck you know my name? I just walked in. Oh, so ya'll can't say shit to me but you can tell this fucker all my damn business! See this that shit I be talkin bout"

Dr. Black lifts her left eyebrow and squints her eyes as she shoots me a dirty look that reminds me of one my mama used to give me just before she said

"Little girl if you don't calm ya ass down"

She began to speak calmly in a low tone.

"Karen I'm going to give you two choices. You can either sit in my office and talk to me or these nice gentlemen behind me will give you a shot, put you in a jacket and position you in a nice quiet room until you're ready to talk. Make your choice."

"I'll take the office for 600 please. Thank you, ma'am!"

"I thought so. Come with me" We walked into a large room with huge windows.

"Here wipe your face and take a seat". She called in a nurse to tend the wound on my side.

As the nurse reached to touch me I jumped to the side and fell out the chair.

"It's ok. No one here will hurt you. I promise" Dr. Black said.

The nurse helped me to my feet as another nurse brought in a clean white t-shirt. I took my torn shirt off and allowed the her to bandage my wound. Dr. Black walked around me looking at all the other marks on my body. When the nurse finished, I put my new shirt on and sat back in the chair with my head hanging low.

"Tell me what happened to you. How did you end up here?"

I wrestled with how much of the story to tell or if I should say anything at all. All of a sudden my emotions began to erupt again. Tears pouring down my face as I began

"I was gon' be quiet but you know what I'm tired of keeping my mouth closed while everybody do what the fuck they want to me. I'm gon' kill all them sons of bitches the simple bastards!!! They wanna fuck me like they crazy while they treat me like shit and tell me they love me while they pray that Jesus blesses us all. Bitch Ima be ya blessing today cause we all gon' meet Him tonight!!! I'm tired... I'm beyond tired. I've been a garbage dump for too long and I'm tired!"

"WOW you got too much going on for us to work through this tonight so what I'm going to do is give you an assignment. I want you to write a letter to your abusers. I'm not going to read it but I do want you to share it with me tomorrow when we meet. I need you to get all of this off your chest. I need you to have no filter with it just like you don't have one with me right now. I'm on call all night so if you need me have somebody page me. But, I want to start with that letter bright and early in the morning."

"So, after I write this letter you gon' let me outta here?"

"I can't promise you'll get out tomorrow but I know you're not crazy. So, I need you to work with me so we can get you out of here. I'm going to have you put in a private room at least for tonight."

She makes a call and within minutes a nurse and one of the Debo looking dudes enters the office to escort me to my room. As I'm leaving Dr. Black says

"We're going to give you something to help you sleep tonight so when you're ready let the nurse know".

"Yes ma'am" I replied as I left. Alone in my room I sat Indian style on the bed and began my letter

Dear Abusers,

My therapist wants me to write this letter so I can get my feelings out. She said she's not going to read it but I have to share it with her. So, what I'm gon' do is tell her what I know she needs to hear so they can let me up outta here. But Ima tell ya'll the truth. Right now, I'm a homicidal maniac and all ya'll are in my line of fire. I'm coming for you! But you won't see it just like I didn't see you. I'm coming like a thief in the night. What I'm gon' do to you will leave you breathless… Wait for it! But what I'm gon' do right now is pray for ya'll because I'm not really sure there is a God but if there is…ya'll gon' need Him. So, here it goes…I hope you receive it because it might be the last prayer you get.

Dear God,

Forgive them for they know not what they've done…

Other Books By Arketa Williams

Get Connected

Facebook.com/AuthorArketaWilliams
Instagram.com/arketawilliams

A Sinner's Circle

226